ABOUT THE TRANSLATOR

CHRISTINA PRIBICHEVICH ZORIĆ has translated more than thirty novels and short-story collections from Bosnian/Croatian/Serbian and French. Her translations include the award-winning *Dictionary of the Khazars* by Milorad Pavić – as well as Pavić's *Last Love in Constantinople* for Peter Owen – and the international best-seller *Zlata's Diary* by Zlata Filipović. She has worked as a broadcaster for the English Service of Radio Yugoslavia in Belgrade and for the BBC in London and was the Chief of Conference and Language Services for the UN International Criminal Tribunal for the Former Yugoslavia in The Hague.

OTHER TITLES IN
THE WORLD SERIES
SERBIAN SEASON

Mirjana Novaković, *Fear and His Servant* (translated by Terence McEneny)

Dana Todorović, *The Tragic Fate of Moritz Tóth* (translated by the author)

PETER OWEN WORLD SERIES

'*The world is a book, and those who do not travel read only one page,*' wrote St Augustine. Journey with us to explore outstanding contemporary literature translated into English for the first time. Read a single book in each season – which will focus on a different country or region every time – or try all three and experience the range and diversity to be found in contemporary literature from across the globe.

Read the world – three books at a time

3 works of literature in
2 seasons each year from
1 country each season

For information on forthcoming seasons go to
peterowen.com / istrosbooks.com

THE HOUSE OF
REMEMBERING
AND
FORGETTING

Filip David

THE HOUSE OF REMEMBERING AND FORGETTING

Translated from the Serbian by
Christina Pribichevich Zorić

With a foreword by Dejan Djokić

PETER OWEN
WORLD SERIES

WORLD SERIES SEASON 3 : SERBIA
THE WORLD SERIES IS A JOINT INITIATIVE BETWEEN
PETER OWEN PUBLISHERS AND ISTROS BOOKS

Peter Owen Publishers / Istros Books
Conway Hall, 25 Red Lion Square, London WC1R 4RL, UK

Peter Owen and Istros Books are distributed in the USA and Canada by
Independent Publishers Group/Trafalgar Square
814 North Franklin Street, Chicago, IL 60610, USA

Translated from the Serbian *Kuća sećanja i zaborava*; first English-language
edition published by Geopoetika Publishing, Belgrade, Serbia, 2015

Paperback ISBN   978-0-7206-1973-7
Epub ISBN   978-0-7206-1974-4
Mobipocket ISBN   978-0-7206-1975-1
PDF ISBN   978-0-7206-1976-8

A catalogue record for this book is available from the British Library.

Cover design: Davor Pukljak, frontispis.hr
Typeset by Octavo Smith Publishing Services

Printed by Printfinder, Riga, Latvia

'And finally, being everybody or anybody, he will appear before us as if he is Nobody in particular. And this takes us to his first trick, to doubt in his very existence.'

Denis de Rougemont, *The Devil's Share*

'Suddenly you discover that you're gone. That you've been broken into a thousand pieces, and that each piece has an eye, a nose, an ear . . . A heap of fragments.'

Lyudmila Ulitskaya*, The People of Our Tsar*

'There are only two ways to live your life. One is as though nothing is a miracle. The other is as though everything is a miracle.'

Albert Einstein

INTRODUCTION

by Dejan Djokić

Filip David's *The House of Remembering and Forgetting*, which in 2014 won the NIN prize (Serbia's major literary award) for best novel of the year, is his first book to appear in English translation. The main protagonist is Albert Weisz, a Holocaust survivor haunted by memories of a tragic family loss and traumas of his own subsequent quest for survival during the Second World War in occupied Yugoslavia. Together with several friends and fellow survivors, Albert struggles to make sense of what happened until, during a visit to New York, he chances upon a mysterious house, with its Remembering Room and its Forgetting Room, where his family history is displayed in front of him. Weisz's character is in some important ways based on David, whose book may be described as a mix of a semi-fictional autobiography and a collective biography of European Jews in the twentieth century. The novel is set in two time frames: the present-day, in the aftermath of the Yugoslav Wars of the 1990s, and during the Second World War. A seemingly fragmented structure is eventually brought together into a powerful, deeply moving story of loss and identity, of being torn between traumatic memories and a fear of forgetting. This is a universal story, and it is also a Holocaust story situated in the specific context of German-occupied Serbia and Yugoslavia.

David was born in 1940, in the central Serbian town of Kragujevac, a year before the Kingdom of Yugoslavia would be occupied and partitioned by Nazi Germany, Fascist Italy and their revisionist collaborators outside and inside the country. His mother's family were Sephardim, descendants of Jews expelled from the Iberian Peninsula in the fifteenth century, who found refuge in the Ottoman Empire, of which Serbia was then a part. The Sephardim kept their Jewish tradition and an archaic form of the Spanish language – Judeo-Spanish or Ladino – and many prospered in the Muslim-dominated empire. They lived in relatively large numbers in urban centres across the Balkans, including Sarajevo, where David's Galician-born father grew up. The Sarajevo Davids belonged to an eminent Ashkenazi Jewish family whose members lived through-out Habsburg-controlled Europe including Vienna – Sigmund Freud was a distant relative. Not unlike other Ashkenazim, David's paternal grandparents looked down on the Sephardim, and it was no surprise that they initially disapproved of their future daughter-in-law. Overcoming family resistance, the young couple married and eventually settled in Sremska Mitrovica, north-west of Belgrade, after David's father was appointed a local judge there on the eve of the invasion of Yugoslavia in April 1941.

The changing political map of 'Turkey-in-Europe' during the course of the long nineteenth century threatened the Empire's long-established, pre-national plural communities, which had tended to co-exist more or less peacefully. The emergence of Christian nation-states, whose elites believed that they could only be in Europe by eliminating 'Turkey' (although a considerable degree of tolerance was displayed towards a 'Turkish', that is, authoritarian, form of ruling), led to the mass emigration of Muslims, most of whom were local converts to Islam rather than ethnic

Turks. Protection of minority rights was one of the conditions for the international recognition of several Balkan states, Serbia among them, at the 1878 Congress of Berlin. While Serbian Jews remained, Serbian-speaking Muslims left to be replaced by Christian and Jewish migrants from neighbouring Habsburg and Ottoman provinces. Serbia, therefore, was a new state in more than one way, and the Jews played a prominent role in the creation of the modern Serbian society. By the early twentieth century they had been fully integrated, some declaring themselves 'Serbs of Moses' faith', and they regarded Serbian to be their mother tongue; among them was the Judić family of Filip David's mother. Meanwhile, philo-Semitism developed among Serbs, especially after the 1912–13 Balkan Wars and the First World War, in which Serbian Jewish officers and soldiers participated with distinction, many losing their lives in battle.

To be sure, anti-Jewish prejudice existed in Serbia, including in some Orthodox Church circles and among conservative intellectuals influenced by Western European anti-Semitic ideas. However, anti-Semitism in Serbia was neither as widespread nor as deep as it was in Central Europe, with no pogroms taking place, unlike in Poland and Russia. The same was true of inter-war Yugoslavia, despite the authorities adopting in late 1940, under Nazi pressure, two anti-Semitic laws reducing Jewish rights. In the 1930s Serbian academics supported their German-Jewish colleagues by publishing their work – including texts by the philosopher Husserl – and offering teaching posts in some cases; this resembled, although never matched in scale, support previously offered to refugees from the Russian Revolution. During this period Yugoslavia facilitated the transit of some 55,000 Jewish refugees from Central Europe to Palestine. Around a thousand were still awaiting Britain's permission to continue the journey when Yugoslavia was invaded; all would perish, together with the majority of local Jews. Out of some 70,000 to 80,000 Jews living in Yugoslavia before the war, just 12,500 to 15,000 survived. Nearly two-thirds of the survivors would emigrate to Israel, although David's parents were not among them. The novel thus also tells the story of a community that all but disappeared in the mid twentieth century.

After the partition of Yugoslavia, a rump Serbia was placed under German military occupation, and a quisling administration was established during the summer of 1941. The Government of National Salvation was without popular legitimacy and enjoyed limited power, and some of its German masters were unconvinced by its usefulness. Its police and a small military force were largely ineffective in fighting the resistance and became increasingly demoralized as the war went on. An influx of Serb refugees from Bosnia and Croatia who fled the Ustaša Terror created additional problems and added to a sense of powerlessness; although, curiously, it was the Communists, Jews and the government-in-exile who were blamed by the quislings for what was quickly turning into a national catastrophe. The collaborationist government did not even exercise authority across all of an already reduced Serbia, the Banat region enjoying a special status because of its large German minority (the *Volksdeutsche*) living there. Nevertheless, leading Serbian collaborators shared National-Socialist values, including anti-Semitism, while Serb quislings indirectly participated in the Holocaust by helping to identify and round up local Jews. There were 'ordinary' Serbs who risked their lives to protect and shelter their Jewish neighbours, as this novel shows, but some were complicit in the Holocaust, even if the Germans carried out the killing. The history of Yugoslavia in the Second World War remains under-researched, with questions of collaboration, complicity in the murder of Jews and other innocent civilians and of resistance and civil war still being subjects of much controversy and little genuine debate.

The Holocaust in Serbia occupies a place on the margins of a vast Western literature on the Second World War, and it does not fit into the pattern of systematic killing of Eastern European Jewry. It was the *Wehrmacht*, the regular German army, that carried out the majority of the killing, not the *SS Einsatzgruppen*, as was the case in occupied Poland and the Soviet Union. German army officers in Serbia tended to be former Habsburg army personnel who had already fought against the Serbs in the First World War – which, of course, began with Austria-Hungary's declaration of war on Serbia in the aftermath of the Sarajevo assassination and ultimately resulted in the dissolution of the dual monarchy. The *Wehrmacht* officers' hostility towards the local population therefore required little encouragement from the Führer, himself a former Habsburg soldier, and the leadership in Berlin.

The killings started soon after the occupation, as part of a policy of reprisals for acts of resistance (the question of who actually resisted – the Communist-led Partisans or the royalist Četniks or both – is also one of the ongoing controversies). The prime targets of German reprisals were Communists and Jews – although often there was no distinction in the eyes of the occupier – but Serb and Roma civilians were also used as hostages. While Serbs would sometimes survive when no Communist connection could be established, no such escape route existed for Serbian Jews. Initially, Jewish men were taken hostage and executed – women, children and the elderly were at this point mostly used for slave labour. After the uprising in Serbia was defeated in late 1941 (and a civil war between the Partisans and Četniks escalated), the remaining Jews, regardless of gender and age, were sent to death camps or killed in a specially designed gas van. The German occupation authorities in Serbia did not merely take part in the Final Solution, by carrying out a systematic murder of Jews independently of Berlin they had in fact anticipated it by several months. Believing – wrongly, as it turned out – that all the Jews were exterminated, they proclaimed Serbia *Judenfrei* in early 1942. Most members of David's maternal family were killed in the infamous Kragujevac massacre of October 1941, when German soldiers shot nearly 2,800 Serbs, Jews and Roma (rounded up with the help of Serb collaborators) in a single day; this was the largest but not the only such mass killing of civilians in Serbia during the autumn of 1941. Meanwhile in Sarajevo the Ustaše would murder around forty-five members of David's extended family.

David and his parents found themselves in Sremska Mitrovica at the beginning of the war and were perhaps saved by the confusion of the early days of the establishment of the Ustaše-run independent Croatia – which stretched almost as far as Belgrade – and the presence of rival Hungarian and German occupation forces in the region. Judge David immediately lost his job, but the family was saved by a *Volksdeutscher*; this had contacts with local Communists who helped David's father join the Partisan resistance. He would frequently visit his wife and two small children – David's brother Miša was born in 1942 – who assumed a Serbian identity and were sheltered by a Serbian farmer. An entire village kept the secret, made easier by the enemy's belief that there were no Jews left alive in the area. Yet this did not mean that they were safe. Young Filip David – now known as Fića Kalinić – survived because of his love of cherries: exhausted by a long march and unable to walk any further, he was about to be shot by an Ustaša soldier but found additional strength to continue when his mother told him a cherry tree awaited at the destination as a reward for those who arrived first (David would write a short story about this experience after the war). On another occasion a Partisan commander asked David's mother to strangle her son because his crying threatened to reveal their hiding place. His parents refused, taking their two small children away from the rest of the group and somehow finding a way to safety; the others were less fortunate and failed to get through the German encirclement.

After the war David started writing, eventually becoming one of the leading young authors in the country. His works gained praise from, among others, Ivo Andrić, the sole Yugoslav winner of the Nobel Prize for Literature. With three other contemporaries – Danilo Kiš, Mirko Kovač and Borislav Pekić – David was part of an informal writers' *kruzhok*. They kept regular correspondence after Pekić, Kiš and eventually Kovač left Belgrade, where David continues to live to this day. Independent-minded intellectuals, the four writers inevitably clashed with the authorities, and yet all four were published to high acclaim and received major national literary prizes – perhaps an example of the peculiarity of former Yugoslavia. In the late 1980s, as post-Tito Yugoslavia entered its final crisis, David founded an independent writers' union in Sarajevo, while, during the 1990s, he would help found and emerge as one of the most eminent members of a small Belgrade circle of anti-war intellectuals. He has been a vocal opponent and a consistent critic of anti-Semitism and nationalism more generally, an engaged intellectual and a leading voice for democracy and reconciliation in former Yugoslavia. The latter is alluded to in the book, which opens with a conference on 'Crimes, Reconciliation, Forgetting' at the Hotel Park in Belgrade in 2004. The only time I saw Filip David in person was at a similar event a few years ago in central Belgrade convened by a German foundation to discuss ways of remembering and commemorating the Holocaust in Serbia. He was one of the most impressive speakers at the conference.

The House of Remembering and Forgetting has a strong auto-biographical element: Sigmund Freud was David's distant relative on his father's side, and a relationship between Freud and the family of David's fictional hero Albert Weisz is alluded to in the novel. Weisz is also related to the great magician Houdini (whose real name was Erik Weisz), a probable metaphor for David and his family's several near-miraculous escapes during the Second World War. Like David, Weisz and his friends in the novel survive the Holocaust thanks to their parents' sacrifice and the humanity of non-Jews, local Germans and Serbs. Unlike Weisz's parents, David survived the war, and, unlike Weisz's mother, they did not throw their younger son from a concentration-camp-bound train in the hope that he might survive. However, leaving children in the care of non-Jewish neighbours and sometimes complete strangers before being taken away to a camp was not uncommon among Serbian Jews. And it is easy to imagine that Filip David understands only too well the ghosts of the past haunting Albert Weisz and other main characters in the book.

This is an original, powerful novel in which David skilfully leads his reader through a complex narrative until its fragments come together in an emotional finale. The story that he tells is a highly personal one and specific to its geographical context, but it is also a universal tale of the human survival instinct in the face of evil and a need to remember and make sense of it all, however tempting it may be to forget those painful memories. *The House of Remembering and Forgetting* is a wonderful book that deserves a wide readership which this edition will, hopefully, bring.

Dejan Djokić
Professor of History at Goldsmiths
University of London
2017

Further reading

Almuli, Jaša, *Živi i mrtvi: Razgovori sa Jevrejima* (The Living and the Dead: Conversations with Jews), Belgrade, 2002

Browning, Christopher R., *Fateful Months: Essays on the Emergence of the Final Solution*, New York, 1985

Byford, Jovan, *Staro Sajmište: Mesto sećanja, zaborava i sporenja* (Staro Sajmište: A Site Remembered, Forgotten, Contested), Belgrade, 2011; available online at https://rs.boell.org/sites/default/files/staro_sajmiste_-_jovan_bajford_72_dpi.pdf

Goldstein, Ivo, 'The Jews in Yugoslavia, 1918–1941: Antisemitism and the Struggle for Equality', n.d., paper available online at http://web.ceu.hu/jewishstudies/pdf/02_goldstein.pdf

Koljanin, Milan, *Jevreji i antisemitizam u kraljevini Jugoslaviji 1918–1941* (Jews and Antisemitism in the Kingdom of Yugoslavia), Belgrade, 2008

Lebl, Ženi, *Dnevnik jedne Judite: Beograd, 1941* (Judita's Diary), Gornji Milanovac, 1990

Manoschek, Walter, *'Serbien ist Judenfrei!'* ('Serbia Is Free of Jews!'), Munich, 1993

Pavlowitch, Stevan K., *Hitler's New Disorder: The Second World War in Yugoslavia*, London, 2008

Ristović, Milan, 'Yugoslav Jews Fleeing the Holocaust, 1941–1945', in John
    K. Roth, Elisabeth Maxwell, Margot Levy and Wendy Whitworth
    (eds), *Remembering for the Future: The Holocaust in an Age of
    Genocide. Vol. 1: History*, Basingstoke, 2001, pp. 512–26
Rochlitz, Imre (with Joseph Rochlitz), *Accident of Fate: A Personal
    Account, 1938–1945*, Waterloo, Ontario, 2011
Rock, Jonna, 'Sarajevo and the Sarajevo Sephardim', *Nationalities Papers*,
    forthcoming
Special issues of *Serbian Studies: Journal of the North American Society
    for Serbian Studies*, dedicated to Jewish experiences in Serbia (Vol. 27,
    Nos 1–2, 2013 and Vol. 28, Nos 1–2, 2017)
Yeomans, Rory (ed.), *The Utopia of Terror: Life and Death in Wartime
    Croatia*, Rochester, New York, 2015

THE NOISE

That sound . . . it kept recurring. A moving train. The wheels of a moving train. At first I couldn't tell where the noise was coming from. It woke me in the dead of night. I got out of bed, opened the window and peered out into the darkness, trying to locate the source. There were no tracks or railway stations anywhere near by.

I put my hands over my ears. I pushed my head under the pillow. Nothing helped. That steady, rhythmic noise would not go away.

Da-da-Dum-da-da-Dum-da-da-Dum.

I dressed, left the house and roamed the deserted streets hoping to get as far away as I could from the monotonous sound of that moving train.

But the sound followed me. It was with me, inside me, unrelenting. It was driving me mad.

Da-da-Dum-da-da-da-Dum.

Then suddenly it stopped. Yet I knew it would return. Each time that much louder, that much more insistent, that much more unbearable.

INTRODUCTION

From the Diary of
Albert Weisz

In which he talks about a chance encounter and whether our fate is predetermined, explains what a daemon is and draws a few conclusions about some of life's misapprehensions

At the beginning of 2004 I took part in an international event at the Park Hotel in Belgrade organized by the European Union and held under the title 'Crimes, Reconciliation, Forgetting'. As with many such gatherings, the tone was largely academic. Most of the time was taken up with futile attempts to define the actual nature of evil and its philosophical, theological, even human essence. We call many things evil, from natural disasters and diseases to violent death, war and crime, but when it comes to evil itself, it is usually the banality of evil that is repeatedly invoked, the thesis that Hannah Arendt set out in the wake of the Eichmann trial in Jerusalem. Many of the speakers said that having reached her conclusion, Ms Arendt could finally sleep soundly in the conviction that a crime of the magnitude of the Holocaust would never happen again, which might not be the case were evil something metaphysical, beyond human conception. As the various speakers read out their papers, I noticed a man sitting in the back row, listening attentively, although he was not one of the participants.

The interesting conversations we had over dinner in the Park

Hotel's spacious dining-room were much more relaxed than the discussions at the conference because most of us knew each other from the days when we lived in what had once been our common country, Yugoslavia; we shared memories, even friendships. There were gruesome stories, told almost anecdotally, about the criminals, murderers and thieves who had been released from prison and gone to the front to fight, about neighbours who had slaughtered each other in the fanatic surge of newfound religious and national hatreds. The evil wrought was attributed to a criminal past or bigotry, to a bad upbringing and poor education, to character faults, to a mentality steeped in tradition, to political manipulation, in other words to all the things that are inherent, not alien, to human nature. The running thread through all these stories was that evil is something base, vulgar, something truly banal and explicable.

'*To understand is to justify,*' a voice said, objecting to the general tone of the conversation. 'These are the words of a great writer who suffered the terrible effects of evil and criminality and who said that a new language would have to be invented to discuss evil, because our way of talking and thinking about it cannot express its full depth.'

The room fell silent for a moment. I saw that the person speaking was the stranger who had been at the back of the conference room.

'I come uninvited to these gatherings to hear all sorts of interpretations because I want to understand the nature and power of a crime that leaves us defenceless, helpless in the face of its unrelenting force.'

Somewhere else his words might have sounded inappropriate, tragicomic even, but the man spoke calmly, with a mesmerizing self-assurance that stilled the room, at least momentarily, and sparked the audience's attention.

He went on, 'I wish it were as simple as some of today's papers make it sound: that evil and crime are merely the work of criminal characters, criminal ideologies, people who have been manipulated, rabid fanatics. If only I could convince myself of what Hannah Arendt believed, maybe I'd be able to get a good night's sleep myself. But my nights are just one continuous, terrible nightmare, because such claims are unproven and uncorroborated; they merely feed our illusion that we have brought the crime under control because we have given it a purely human face.'

Just then a waiter appeared with a fresh round of drinks, and the audience started losing interest in the man. The noise level rose again, and, as often happens at gatherings like this, somebody made a rude joke about the uninvited guest, and people stopped listening to him. As I was closest, the man then turned to me, determined to find at least one person who would hear him out.

'The first time I thought about the actual nature of crime was when I was a boy and had to face the horror of unimaginable, unfair, senseless – whatever you want to call it – dying. You know, some people live all their lives without ever having seen a dead person, while others are suffocated by the constant presence of death in their lives and their dreams. I was ten years old when the Second World War broke out. I lived with my parents in a small provincial Serbian town occupied by the Germans. A family of *Volksdeutsche*, ethnic Germans, moved into our house. They had a son who was a bit older than me. We started spending time together. One day he told me that my father had been arrested and would be executed that same afternoon along with the other hostages. I told my mother. She said, "That's just childish rubbish, your father will be released." But my new friend grabbed my hand and said, "I never lie. I heard it from my father. C'mon, you can see for yourself!" He took me to the courtyard of a former factory where we hid behind a mound of earth. We didn't have long to wait. The Germans set up two heavy machine-guns, and then a group of people, their hands tied, was led out of the shed. I recognized my father among them. The Germans shot them before our very eyes. I saw my father drop. He was a strong, tall man in his prime; he had never been sick a day in his life. The memory of his senseless death stayed with me all throughout my childhood and youth. It was the most awful feeling, to realize that such a crime could be committed for no reason, that death could strike somebody down, somebody who'd been chosen at random out of thousands of people, somebody who was simply picked up off the street. He didn't know his killers, and they didn't know him; it was an utterly absurd, terrible crime. I lost the power of speech that day; it took a long time for me to start talking again, and it was only thanks to the support of my mother and the care and love of my younger sister.'

Fresh bottles of wine kept arriving at the table, and the noise level increased. Everybody forgot about the uninvited guest except for me, and I, partly out of curiosity and partly out of politeness, went on listening to his story.

'Now, in hindsight, I can see that that tragic event was fateful, it seared itself into my mind and was to mark the rest of my life. You see, that is what I am trying to show you people – you who take a theoretical approach to crime and punishment, victim and executioner – that these things cannot be fully understood based only on reason or emotions, that there is something above and beyond that. The ancient Greeks called this "guide that walks beside us and remembers our life's purpose" a daemon.'

Here the man stopped for a moment, then continued, 'An

unknowable, non-human, non-material being lives secretly inside every person and rules their destiny. My mother was taken to a camp where she died without ever seeing the face of her killers. Her death, too, was anonymous. Like the violent death of my sister, who was killed on Liberation Day in a frenzied attack by a combatant who'd had a nervous breakdown and started murdering everybody in sight. Not so long ago, I lost my daughter. She was shot dead by a sniper in Sarajevo. One cannot talk about the banality of the crime, sir. One can talk about the daemon who for some is a guardian angel and for others a judge and executioner; one can talk about the workings of something powerful and untouchable, something we are unable to interpret. I am convinced that every individual, every family, indeed entire peoples, have just such a mysterious power watching them, a power called a daemon. It guides them, it saves them or it destroys them. How can people talk about the banality of evil when all these deaths, the deaths of my own nearest and dearest but also of so many others, even though meted out by humans, are really the work of faceless killers, of anonymous executioners who didn't even know their victims? Unlike Mrs Arendt, whose theory about the banality of evil is accepted here, I am convinced that evil is cosmic, irrational, unrestrainable. Debates about sin, punishment, forgiveness, solace are all pointless, all false.'

I saw tears gather in the corners of his eyes. He wiped them away with his hand. I wanted to say something, to express my belated condolences, but nothing came out of my mouth. He, meanwhile, seemed embarrassed by what he had said. He stood up, turned away and without saying goodbye walked out. I didn't even have time to ask him his name; we hadn't been introduced.

With time, maybe I would have forgotten about the man and

his story, but something happened that jogged my memory. The other day I saw a news report on television about a bomb attack carried out by some deranged person on a busload of passengers. They showed pictures of the dead. In one of them I recognized the man who had spoken to me that evening about the merciless, aggressive daemon, the mythical being who connects us to the other world.

Will we ever really know anything more about this hidden, mysterious herald of life and death, this angel of salvation and angel of destruction who from the deepest shadows determines our fate?

ALBERT'S DREAM

Albert has a disturbing dream.

He is at a lonely provincial train station. The stationmaster's house is run down, the plaster peeling. Through the two dirty windows you can just about make out the faces of the station staff. They are the ugly old faces of haggard postal and railway workers.

Everything is steeped in menacing semi-darkness. The sky is grey, the surrounding fields shrouded in mist.

Albert is standing on the platform, waiting. He does not know what or who he is waiting for.

Suddenly, a behemoth with two glowing red eyes emerges from the gloom. The black locomotive is pulling a dozen carriages. The only sound to be heard is the clattering of the wheels. It strikes fear in Albert. Panic, even. He wants to run away from the platform. He doesn't even know how he got there. But he can't move.

There are no lights on in the carriages.

The train slows down as it comes to the station but does not stop. Albert can see the faces pressed against the carriage windows. They are not the faces of the living.

They are the dead, and this is their train.

Rising above the relentless noise that strikes both terror and horror in his soul is a voice, a child's voice.

'Brother, save me! It is so dark here!'

It is the voice of Albert's little brother Elijah.

Albert cries out, 'Don't be afraid, Eli, I'm here!'

But all he can do is watch the train vanish into the night.

He wakes up in a cold sweat.

ONE

From the Diary of
Albert Weisz

*Which is devoted to thoughts about the limits of the
permissible and attempts to exceed them*

I filled pages and pages in my diary; there were periods when I
wrote night after night, driven by what I can only call a mad kind
of energy. I put down the wildest thoughts, the strangest testi-
monies and experiences, which, I felt, brought me closer to
explaining the meaning of everything we had been through. And
just when I thought that I was emerging from that dark, complicated
labyrinth, that I was getting closer to understanding the secret
mechanism of its tangled paths, all the passageways suddenly
started closing themselves off, my hand failed me, my thoughts
turned into chaotic non-sequiturs. I stopped writing, recording,
witnessing; I was no longer able to formulate a single coherent
thought. What I penned on the white paper during the day erased
itself, disappeared at night, as if it had never been there. At times,
in moments of inspiration, I would imagine that I was writing
'black fire on white fire', the way the mystical Torah was written.
God forbid that I should compare myself to the mysterious writer
of a text that is so much more than just a text, that is life itself,
existence for and of itself, a living organism that contains the

reason for its own being. Sometimes I felt that the words I was writing were leaving a fiery mark, painful burns on my hands, which, the ancient manuscripts tell us, sometimes happened to the inquisitive who, insufficiently prepared, tried to discover the learning and secrets of higher powers.

Afraid that I had crossed the line of the permissible, I would leave parts of the manuscript unfinished and scattered. I would stop writing, put what I had penned in the pantry, which was already full of similar piles of paper. I would keep these pages there for days, sometimes longer, keep them from whom? From myself? I don't know. All I know is that when I looked through them again what I found were mostly illegible, confused texts. Something had happened in the interim. I swear, I discovered comments written in a handwriting like mine, which, I guess, was meant to confuse me and make me think that I was losing my mind and going mad. The message, I'm sure, was supposed to be that there are areas one is not permitted to enter, areas overseen by powers greater than those of humans.

There were moments when my hand stopped of its own accord and my mind became muddled. I would feel listless and could barely stand up without holding on to something for support; the ground would sway under my feet; I would feel faint. The strange illness would dispatch me to my bed, my head a mess. I tried to seize control of my own devastated mind, not understanding what was happening to me or why.

The doctors were unable to diagnose my illness. The symptoms: fainting spells, high fever, aches and pains in every part of my body, cautionary, troubled, bad dreams, a voice that only I could hear, menacing, warning, telling me to stop writing.

I am trying to discover why humankind has experienced such

misery, how it is that one can move from a quiet, orderly life to troubled, disturbed times, where life loses all value. Where does this evil come from, where does it hide before it sends everything to rack and ruin and then retreats, leaving devastation in its wake and in people's hearts?

I fight this feeling of desperate helplessness and inner panic by trying to relax and by closing my eyes. I inhale through both nostrils, imagining the air coursing through my body, filling it with fresh energy. I apply what are called 'simple breathing exercises' from a point far off in the distance, from the edge of the universe. And then I feel relief, not for long, but relief all the same.

Some things, it seems, and I increasingly believe, must not and cannot be put in writing. Not because nobody wants to, but because it is not permitted. It is not human will-power that does not permit it, but rather a will-power capable of stopping the hand that writes, the head that thinks, a power that is stronger than all that we are, ever were or shall be.

TWO

Dedicated to the memory of my father
and his prophetic vision

My earliest memories stretch far back into the past. Etched in my mind is the stern but honest face of my grandfather, a Polish rabbi from what was then called Lemberg and is today Lviv. My father did not follow in his footsteps; he was one of those enlightened Jews who renounced tradition, spoke Polish, Russian and German and were ashamed of Yiddish as the language of Central Europe's Jewish poor. He met my mother quite by chance while travelling through Siberia. Her family was Sephardi. They were the Jews expelled from Spain who spoke Ladino, a mixture of Old Spanish and Slavic words. Her father had a shop in K. It was a big family, with nine children. Holding place of honour in the glass-door cabinet, among the porcelain plates, next to the menorah with its mother-of-pearl base, was a big, heavy key, an ancient family relic passed on from generation to generation. It was the key to the gate of the house in Seville, which the Berahis, our maternal ancestors, had been forced to leave under threat of the Inquisition established by Queen Isabella. The key represented a by-now dimmed yearning for Spain and had been kept in memory of the story of young Simon

Berahi. Shipwrecked, Simon stepped foot on Mediterranean soil and joined a group of pilgrims. He travelled with them from one holy place to another, had all sorts of adventures and listened to wonderful tales that were retold down the generations as legends that combined real events and Kabbalistic allegories. They told of long years of wandering, of exile, of having no home to call your own, of a life that keeps reminding us that we are merely guests in a foreign world.

My parents met in the 1920s, and, as fate would have it, their chance encounter at a family gathering was to determine the rest of their lives. Marriages between the Ashkenazim and Sephardim were rare. The Ashkenazim represented, as in the case of my father, the Jewish aristocracy, whereas the Sephardim, once a proud part of Spanish culture, had over time come to typify the Balkan and Jewish poor.

My father was distantly related to the famous Houdini, whose real name was Erik Weisz. He was one of Rabbi Mayer Weisz's six children. The great illusionist became famous for his escape acts from locked spaces and chains, displaying skills that verged on the impossible. My father often joked, although later said quite seriously, that this was a legacy shared by all the Weiszes.

One of my father's close relatives was named Erik after the celebrated escapologist. He was one of the few members of the Weisz family to have survived the Holocaust, although later he disappeared without a trace. According to unconfirmed rumours, he finished up in a mental asylum.

In 1937 my father went on a business trip to Austria and Germany. He returned a very worried man. Hitler had already taken power, and the Nazis had passed their race laws. The events that followed were unstoppable.

My father said that the world around us was closing in on itself, that it was becoming dangerous and that he, as head of the family, had to find a way to save and protect us. His picture of an orderly world fell apart. None of what happened could have occurred in a world based on natural and social laws. He had a clear vision of the evil hurtling our way. A world believed to be orderly, with certain inviolable values, found itself on the brink of collapse, of extinction. The evil spread rapidly; there was hardly any time to do anything. Suddenly everything had changed. Many people did not understand how or why.

Our lives are all interconnected, even when we do not wish it. The whole world is just one big book, composed of a multitude of words, and those words had become jumbled. Anyone able to discover and read their real, true meaning could see the full horror of what was to come. Dr Freud called it 'the frightening normality of evil'. It is no accident that I mention the good doctor. My paternal grandmother's last name was Freud, and she was a favourite of the famous Viennese therapist.

My father started having second thoughts. Had he placed too much faith in a rational world? Had he been too quick to renounce the teachings of his ancestors? It was becoming increasingly clear that the world was being governed not by rational but by irrational powers. It was plunging irrevocably towards catastrophe, towards what people endowed with a 'third eye' could already see – execution sites, mass killings, whole families separated on their way to the death camps. Yes, I swear to all that I hold sacred that my father's prophetic visions included all these things. His extraordinary gift of being able to see into the future enabled him to reveal, layer by layer, the meaning of what was happening, to reveal the future hidden in the present. Speaking sometimes with conviction, at other times in despair or hope, he told us, my mother and me, that there were other, secret worlds apart from our own, that lives were lived not only in this life but in other, parallel dimensions as well.

Elijah was only two at the time. He did not yet realize the kind of world he was entering. Neither did I, not fully anyway. By the age of six I was convinced that I was already like an adult. My father would proudly say that he knew he could rely on me, and that was very important in such dark and dangerous times. I took it as a great compliment.

My brother Elijah was entrusted to my care. I loved him very much. They taught us that the two of us were one, that I was the elder and must never leave his side, that I must always help him and teach him the important things in life. I took it all very seriously. 'My little big brother,' I whispered, leaning over his bed as I put him to sleep. Elijah was delicate, translucent almost; he was just learning to talk. They say that children who start talking later are smarter, cleverer than other children, that they weigh and assess everything and that when they do start talking they are articulate and speak intelligently.

All the same, I saw the world through the eyes of a child, naïvely believing that everything around me was there to make me feel safe: my parents, relatives and friends, my brother Elijah, things I could touch, the passing of day into night, the changing seasons.

My father's increasingly obvious concern, his moodiness and disjointed sentences signalled a man who was gradually losing touch with his surroundings, dragging us into a dark adventure, separating us from the things we knew and understood, from the world that we belonged to and that belonged to us. Indeed, his behaviour after his trips to Vienna and Berlin poisoned my soul with fear, fear of the unknown. Even today the memory of those days can cause me unbearable distress: had my adored father, whom I unquestioningly believed, suddenly succumbed to some sort of madness while I lived in the dangerous illusion that the visible world I inhabited was stable and unchanging?

I was too young, too inexperienced to understand what lay at the root of these changes in my father, changes that were visible not just to my mother and me but to everyone around us as well.

They stemmed from his concern for our survival. Having understood before many others that a crack had appeared in our world and that it was opening into a yawning abyss, disgorging a darkness of apocalyptic proportions, my father saw himself as our protector, his duty being to find a safe place for us, far removed from any threat. He clearly saw even then what many people were to realize a few years later: the collapse of all that was human. Certainly, it was not just anxiety or worry that plagued him but an inner horror, an inner panic that he could neither suppress nor stop. If madness is to be at odds with 'the experience of collective common sense', then he was indeed mad. But what was this 'collective common sense'? Nothing other than a dangerous illusion. My father's only obsession – let us even call it a mad obsession – was to save us, to rescue us from what was inexorably awaiting us.

What could, what did the few people who saw the impending Armageddon do? Well, there is the true story of a father who, sick with worry, started poisoning his children, first with small doses of Zyklon B then gradually increasing the amount with a view to making the children resistant to the lethal gas. How did the poor man know, several years before the toxic gas was put into use, that it would become an indispensable means of mass destruction? Well, he knew because he had a vision. He was inspired. Some people are able to see events that are yet to occur with such clarity and conviction that they seem to relate to the present, not the future.

There was not much choice. He had to find a safe but sure way for us to disappear, to disappear out of the reach of danger. My mother and I, I must admit, did not believe, but nevertheless accepted, my father's ideas about the various ways one could become invisible or at least so minute as to be imperceptible. My mother half joked that even if we could find a way to effect such a transformation it would still be a dangerous business. It would expose us to a new threat, to the risk of being stepped on, either accidentally or deliberately. In other words, there was still a danger. This angered my father because he detected not only scepticism in my mother's words but also common sense, and he considered that to be absurd and stupid at a time when there was no common sense any more.

Much later I came to see that anything is possible in life and that the most complicated things are often also the simplest.

There are various ways to disappear. One way is to become somebody else. Until yesterday you were Albert Weisz; as of today there is no Albert Weisz, there is somebody else, somebody with a different name who fits neatly into this topsy-turvy world. Once you existed, now you do not. Being a child, I found it a horrifying, frightening thought. It meant losing everything you cared about: parents, friends, yourself.

Later, although not much later, many people achieved a kind of disappearance. On the road of no return to the red-hot ovens of Auschwitz. That was the final destination of a world brought to total collapse.

But my father meant something else by disappearance. He meant absence, non-presence, invisibility. He believed in the power of the mind and the power of the word. Today we can safely say that ours is not a material world. This has been proven by scientists and by the evermore complex laws of physics that delve into the very essence of so-called reality. Today, even celebrated physicists admit that, although they have little to say to one another, they do talk to well-known mystics. Physics has gone beyond the comprehensible and into the field of metaphysics. What we prove today by means of the most advanced instruments, mystics knew and proved by means of intuition. There is scientific evidence that various theoretically verifiable forms of disappearance do exist, and my father tried to apply them in practice. The tragic truth is that he was considerably ahead of his time.

While panic spread and racial laws were promulgated in many countries, we sat in a darkened room like helpless victims waiting for their executioners. At least so it may have seemed to somebody looking in from the outside. One of the first lessons we learned was self-control. We worked on changing ourselves and the reality in which we were living. In truth, my father's goal was to achieve a higher level of consciousness.

'By controlling your mind,' my father said, 'you can control what your inner eye sees. And that means moving to other dimensions of reality where you can find refuge, where you can be safe, hidden, invisible, away from the world where there is no room for us any more, a world where we are at the mercy of all sorts of scum.'

My father lit a candle in the pitch-dark room. Gazing at the flame, we recited the lines of the poem 'When Fear is Like a Rock', by the ancient Spanish poet Shem-Tov ben Joseph ibn Falaquera. If my memory serves me, it went like this:

When fear is like a rock
I become a hammer
When sorrow becomes a flame
I turn myself into the sea
And it is then that
My heart grows strong
Like the moon shining more brightly
When all is cloaked in the blackness of night.

With time we became adept at looking for ways to move from one reality to another. And had there been more time we might have actually done it. But we always had to remember that we could disappear into one of those unknown, unexplored worlds and be swallowed up for ever. And so we learned how to use certain symbols, letters and signs as a way of staying connected to the reality from which we now sought temporary refuge.

The Kabbalah mystic's book says: 'Taking wing is joyful, but before flying one must know how to land.'

I was no expert in these matters; I was lacking in years, faith and experience. The day that I parted from my father, mother and brother, I was not Albert Weisz any more, I was a foreigner in a foreign world, a boy full of fear and hate.

But I will always remember my father's words, 'When you think that all is lost, just close your eyes. It is the quickest road to salvation. There are many other worlds within and outside us, worlds where our persecutors, be they people or demons, cannot find us.'

THREE

'Don't cry, my little one'

Thirsty and hungry, we had been travelling for two days and two nights. We slept on the hard floor, barely managing to squeeze ourselves in among the human bodies cramming the wagon. Elijah would cry, finding comfort in my mother's arms, and she would sing to him softly, to him alone:

> Don't cry, my little one, the Messiah shall come,
> When shall he come?
> Soon he shall come.
> What kind of days shall they be?
> Joyful days, days full of song,
> Days of happiness,
> Hallelujah, my little one!

I believed in my father's ability to find a way out of any threatening situation. He was working on it at that very moment.

Against the noise of the clattering wheels, crying children and despairing adults, my father was carefully carrying out his plan.

Using our bodies as a shield and a knife he had managed to conceal in his boot, he slowly prised loose the wooden boards of the cattle car. My mother wiped the sweat dripping from his face. The work was slow – you could barely see even a chink between the boards – but I knew that my father would succeed. He was not one to give up. After all, coursing through his veins was the blood of the great Houdini, the rabbi's son Erik Weisz, whose escapes had thrilled the world.

By midnight my father had enlarged the opening. I could see the full moon trailing behind us and in its ghostly light the snow-blanketed fields.

'Albert,' he whispered, 'we'll soon be parting company. The two of you will be on your own for a while. Remember everything I've taught you. Take care of Elijah. You are all that he'll have. Take care of our little Elijah,' he said, embracing me. 'We will see each other again, we will be together, in this life or the next.'

He leaned over to kiss me. I saw a tear in his eye. It dropped on to my arm. I can still feel the warm trace that it left.

He waited for the train to slow down. Elijah clung to our mother. She sobbed, but she had no choice. She pushed him away. My father took him. The last thing I remember is Elijah's frantic look. He did not understand what was happening, why he could not stay with us.

My father pushed him out through the opening he had made between the boards. Elijah slid into the night.

'Now you,' he said. I tried to wriggle through the opening, but I couldn't.

My father dug the knife into the wood to enlarge the gap. The minutes ticked by. Somehow I managed to squeeze through. I dropped on to the snow.

I rose to my feet and in the moonlight saw the train moving off, carrying away my beloved parents.

Then I walked along the tracks looking for Elijah. I called out his name, softly at first, then loudly, yelling that I was here, I was coming for him, telling him to shout out. I moved away from the tracks and into the woods, searching for even the smallest sign of him. There was nothing. Silence, a terrible silence engulfed everything around me. I was overcome by fatigue. My voice became fainter. I veered left and right. It was almost morning.

I did not find Elijah. It was a betrayal on more than one level. I had betrayed my beloved brother. I had betrayed my mother and my father. I screamed with pain, alone in the vast whiteness, wanting only to sleep, to die, never to wake up.

FOUR

Which tells the story of Volksdeutsche *Johann Kraft,*
as told to the investigating authorities in N. in 1945

I was born in the small town of N. on the banks of the Danube. That is where I grew up. That is where I got married. I spent my entire life in a house on the outskirts of town. My wife gave me a son, a boy we loved more than anything else in the world. But misfortune hits when you least expect it; it is brutal, sudden and changes your life in a heartbeat. In the spring of 1941 Hans was taking a dip in the river with his friends. As he swam away from the riverbank he got caught up in a whirlpool, and it dragged him down into the water. For days we looked for his body, but we never found him. My Ingrid seemed to lose her mind after that, and maybe she really did. She sat in a corner of the room weeping; then she stopped talking; she withdrew into herself, into the hell that had opened up inside her. It wasn't easy for me either, but life goes on. Some things you simply cannot change or put right.

Now, let me explain that at the time I was a forest ranger. Maybe that helped me to accept things as they are. All day long I would roam the fields and woods, on the lookout for poachers. War was approaching. Most of the people in our little town were ethnic Germans, like Ingrid and me. They called us *Volksdeutsche*. The others could hardly wait for the Germans to come, but to me it was all the same. True, like my fellow Germans I put a picture of the Führer, Adolf Hitler, on the wall next to the icon of St. George. Because I did not hate anybody, my heart was still grieving. When the Germans entered our little town they were warmly welcomed, like brothers. Even before, the town had had the *Kulturbund* for strengthening ties with Germany. The young donned German uniforms and joined the troops of the Wehrmacht. In my own forest-ranger's uniform I served whatever authority came along, including this one. Many things changed, not just who was in power. Everybody was saying that the war was already over, that the Germans had won, but all the same you could feel a lot of uncertainty in the air. I stopped going to the woods so often. It had become dangerous; you no longer knew who you might meet, who might fire a bullet at your head for no reason. Mostly, I walked along the edge of the woods, along the railway tracks, just so as not to be at home with my wife, whose suffering had brought me to the brink of despair because it made me feel so helpless. In addition to the regular train timetable, which I knew by heart, these tracks also serviced trains carrying troops to the front and, from early autumn, cattle cars as well, where you could see people peering out through the cracks trying to shout something, but I would turn away and mind my own business. More and more often I found messages next to the tracks, written in different languages on scraps of paper tossed out of those trains, messages for someone, somewhere. I only ever glanced at them, then crumpled them and tore them up. I had enough troubles of my own. It was not until later that I learned where these trains were going and who they were transporting. But I could not offer help to anybody, and, besides, it was none of my business.

The winter of 1942 saw us buried deep in snow. It was one of those nasty winters when even the game die of hunger and cold. One freezing morning I set out shouldering several bundles of hay for the forest animals, to help them out a little. I didn't have to, but there was nobody else to do it. Anyway, I felt that the forest and its animals had, in a way, been entrusted to my safekeeping.

I came back, as usual, along the railway tracks. At one point I noticed human footprints. I saw at once that they were not an adult's – I knew a thing or two about that. They swerved away towards the unending whiteness of the fields and woods. Night was falling, and whoever it was would never survive the bitter cold. I followed the footprints and soon saw something like a dark blot on the plain where the encroaching evening had already cast its shadow. It was a boy, not more than seven or eight years old, dressed in rags, already blue from the cold. He stopped as soon as he saw me. He obviously had no strength left to run. He was definitely running away from somebody, that was clear. I picked him up and, having no other choice, brought him home.

He shivered in my arms. I could feel his heart beating. It was too late to take him to the police station, so I left it for the next day, knowing that what he urgently needed was to be sat next to a hot stove and warmed up. His lips were blue from the cold, so I wrapped my sheepskin coat around him. Almost inaudibly he mentioned his brother, whispering that he would not go anywhere without him. But, I swear, there was no sign of the other boy anywhere.

I trudged through the deep snow, wanting to get home as quickly as I could. And that is how the story that was to change my life began. I could never have imagined what was to come. And even if, by some miracle, I had, what else could I have done?

I brought the boy into the house. When Ingrid saw us she stood stock still for a second, as if expecting a miracle, as if I were bringing our Hans back home. I told her how I had found the boy in the snow, but she simply turned on her heel and went to her room. The boy was sobbing, tearlessly. I stripped off his clothes, found a pair of Hans's pyjamas, placed him on the bed and wrapped him up in a blanket. I wasn't sure if he would survive; that was in God's hands.

While putting his things away, I found a message sewn into his vest. The boy's name was Albert. His mother asked for whoever found him to help the child. I don't know how she ever managed to throw him off the train. Such things did happen, of course. Mothers found all sorts of ways to save their children. Some threw their children into the river when crossing a bridge or hid them in roadside ditches. These children were discovered sometimes dead, sometimes alive. If the latter, they were put on the next train rumoured to be heading far north to the Polish camps.

I made up a bed for myself right next to his. Around midnight I was awoken by the soft tread of barely audible steps. I am a light sleeper; the slightest sound wakes me up. It was my Ingrid going over to the boy, who was tossing and turning, muttering in his sleep. She lifted her candle and gazed at the child's face in its weak light. She stood quietly like that for several long minutes. I was afraid she was unwell. Just as I was about to call out her name she turned around and tiptoed back to her room. I fell fast asleep, exhausted by the day's events. When I woke up Ingrid was again standing by the boy's bed. His breathing was laboured, his cheeks flushed; he was shivering all over. He obviously had a fever. Ingrid placed damp compresses on his forehead and rubbed him down with homemade brandy. Thick snow was swirling outside. I had meant to take him to the police station that morning, but I had to put it off.

The change in Ingrid surprised me. She, who for months had been so depressed, suddenly pulled herself out of that dark, disturbing dream. She who for so long had not cared about anything was now preoccupied with restoring this little intruder to health. And, for the first time since our son's death, I heard her speak. Admittedly, just a few words, stroking the boy's head as she took the damp compresses off his brow. 'My little Hans, my little boy,' she murmured. Maybe I should have stopped it right then; maybe I should have stepped in and shouted at the top of my lungs that this was not Hans. Who knew where he was from? This was a little Jewish boy from who knows where, a boy I had miraculously saved. But I did none of that. On the contrary, I did everything I could to support her insane belief that this castaway, this lost little boy was our Hans. I did it, may God forgive me and have mercy on my soul, because I wanted to save her from the darkness she lived in, ease the pain of her madness and make her illusion real. And, indeed, when I took a closer look at the poor little boy I noticed, I know what I'm saying here, that he really did look like our Hans. Well then, I said to myself, heaven itself must have sent him to console Ingrid and make our lives bearable.

For a few weeks we did not know if the boy would live or die. He fought his demons and the prospect of death. Ingrid sat by his side night and day. I prayed to God to spare the child because Ingrid would never survive a second loss. We had embarked upon a dangerous adventure. The punishment for hiding Jews, even a lost child found half frozen in the snow, was death. But I didn't think about that at the time. As the child recovered and the snow melted, it was as if nature itself was coming back to life and recovering along with him. Although it was still only the beginning of March, spring was in the air. The boy took his first step out of the house, into the courtyard. Our house was on high ground, and you could see all around – the little town in the valley, the woods on the opposite side of the river and the railway tracks. We had to take care that he did not wander off, because on one occasion he set out across the field towards the tracks, but fortunately we noticed it in time and managed to bring him back. I tried to tell him, without Ingrid hearing, that his mother knew where he was and one day would come to fetch him. But until then he had to be patient and wait. That is how, slowly but surely, I started lying more and more, both to him and to Ingrid. I didn't have a choice. When the boy recovered and put on Hans's suit, when Ingrid combed his hair the way she used to comb Hans's, the boy looked exactly like our son. He was like him in every respect except for one: his behaviour. He showed no love or affection for us, although Ingrid and I gave him both. He would deliberately stomp around in the courtyard, splashing mud over Hans's suit; he would cut his hair with scissors, would not answer to the name of Hans and would refuse to say grace before a meal. Ingrid could not hold back her tears. She had recognized her son in the boy but was hurt and frightened by his refusal to accept her as his real mother. I talked to the boy like an equal, an adult, explaining that we wished only the best for him. Yes, it was a very complicated, sad story. The woman for whom I had built an illusion based on lies believed me, but the boy, still uncorrupted, inexperienced, although precocious, refused to play along. All the same, I lived in the clearly false conviction that I was slowly winning him over; indeed, I was sure of it – until Hans's birthday. I remember the day well: 5 April 1942. Ingrid was so excited. She was up at the crack of dawn, cleaning the house and baking the birthday cake. Then she put on her best dress, unlocked the door to Hans's room and brought Albert, the little Jewish boy, into the room. She pulled opened the curtains, and light flooded the room. All around, on the floor, on the bed, were Hans's things just the way he had left them. I stood at the door, the smell of stale air, dust and rot filling my nostrils, while Ingrid led the boy in. I had a bad feeling. And then the child saw Hans's picture on the wall – it was like looking at himself in the mirror. Dressed the same way, his hair combed the same way. The spitting image of Hans. That was when he realized what he may have only sensed before – that we wanted to turn him into somebody else, somebody whose spirit still inhabited the house, into a replica of our late son. In fact, he was supposed not only to take his place but to become him in every way. But then something happened, something that, despite everything, I did not expect. He exploded with anger and hatred. He started lashing out at everything in the room, like a little savage. He grabbed the picture off the wall, smashed the frame, threw it to the floor and started furiously stamping on the broken pieces of glass. Not a trace of gratitude for everything we had done for him! Ingrid simply did not understand what was happening. She just buried her face in her hands. That was the last straw. I grabbed the boy, roughly I admit, because now I was ready to explode myself, as if he were to blame for Hans's death, for Ingrid's suffering. The boy fought me as best he could, but I overpowered him, dragged him out of the room and locked him in the pantry. 'You're not coming out', I shouted, 'until you apologize for what you've done!'

What upset me the most was that now Ingrid turned against

me. 'What are doing to him? What are you doing?' she yelled. She came up to me. I saw nothing but hatred in her eyes. I was devastated. She even tried to hit me. I grabbed her frail arms, but I had no strength to explain myself or persuade her of anything. I was seized with an uncontrollable desire for revenge. I unlocked the pantry door. 'You piece of scum,' I said to the little Jew. 'Your parents have abandoned you, for ever! They're not coming back for you, not ever!' As soon as the words came out of my mouth I regretted them. But you cannot take back what you have said. I knew I had ruined everything; it was all a mess.

I went into the courtyard, sat on my bicycle and set out for the German Command. I had decided to report the boy, describe how I had found him by the railway tracks and taken pity on him but had quickly seen my mistake when I realized he was a Jewish fugitive. I circled the Command building several times, but I did not report him, I swear I didn't. I did not have the will to do something like that. I cycled aimlessly down the path towards the woods, as far away from home as possible. I stopped under a big oak tree, lay my bike down, sat on the grass and gazed up at the sky. A flock of birds flew over; birds filled the branches of the big oak. Everything was alive, but I felt as if I were dying. The sun was just about to set when I got back on my bike and headed for home.

I don't know if it was a foreboding, but as I neared the house I started feeling increasingly uneasy, afraid, remorseful.

Nobody was there. Not the boy, not Ingrid. My heart sank; the silence in the house filled me with dread.

I went through the dining-room, bedroom, side rooms and came out through the back door that opened on to the courtyard. And there, on the porch, a rope had been thrown over the upper beam and hanging from it was my Ingrid.

She had lost our Hans, and now she had lost obstinate little Albert. She couldn't live with it.

I never saw the boy again. I don't know what happened to him.

I did not report him to the Command, honest I didn't. That's the whole story.

FIVE

*In which Albert Weisz talks about an unusual
book and the miracle it describes*

One of my few remaining pleasures in life is to browse in small
bookshops among the jumble of old and new books. It was in just
such a place on the outskirts of town that I met an old secondhand
dealer with whom I spent hours talking about books. On one of my
visits, he pulled one out of a pile perched haphazardly on the table.

'This arrived today,' he said. 'Do you want a look?'

The book was in good condition. The title was certainly unusual:
Miracles That Occurred in Nazi Camps. The author's name meant
nothing to me: Yisroel Spira, a Hassidic rabbi from Bluzhov.

I took the book, feeling that in some way it was meant for me.
I cannot explain it any other way since I do not believe in chance.
Nothing in this world ever happens by chance.

One of the rabbi's stories was about an incident that happened
in Auschwitz.

I recognized my father from the rabbi's description. He did not
mention him by name, but it was, in every respect, my father! The
dreamer who believes in miracles and is constantly thinking up
ways to get out of hopeless situations.

Fate often toys with human lives, arranging unusual encounters, extraordinary events and situations. And so it was that in Auschwitz my father met the Hassidic rabbi of Bluzhov, Yisroel Spira. Another character who believed in the impossible.

It is a miracle that I ever even walked into the bookshop on the day that this particular book arrived, having passed through who knows how many hands before finding its way into mine.

The event it describes happened on Hanukkah in 1942.

MIRACLE IN AUSCHWITZ

That day, in the camp the rabbi writes about, the SS selected a random group of female inmates, led them out of the barracks, beat them with iron rods and then shot them dead. The massacre lasted from dawn until dusk. The area outside the barracks was strewn with lifeless bodies.

This terrible incident happened on the day of Hanukkah. In the evening the remaining inmates gathered to kindle the light of Hanukkah. In place of a candle, they made a wick out of threads they had pulled from their camp clothes and used black shoe polish for oil. The rabbi of Bluzhov sang three blessings, thanking the King of the Universe for having 'allowed us to live this long'.

When the rabbi's voice fell silent, my father, who was one of the inmates who had witnessed that painful day, went up to the rabbi. He asked him how he could thank God on a day when so many people had been killed. What is the sense of believing in God when millions of innocent people are dying?

In the total darkness that pervaded the room the rabbi lit a candle and told my father to focus on the tiny flame which, when combined with the mystical force of the words, had unimaginable power. The Kabbalah's famous *Zohar, Book of Splendour* says that when contemplating the flame one should see five colours: white, yellow, red, black and sky blue. Concentration is achieved when a ring of sky blue encircles the darkness. However far the darkness spreads, it is always ringed by the same colour, the most beautiful sky blue imaginable. It is at that point that you reach a higher level of consciousness where physical laws cease to apply, where you travel at speeds many times faster than light, where time and space do not exist. The past, the present, the future are all there, all accessible. Your inner eye takes you to worlds that have four or five dimensions. These are dangerous journeys, and, unless you have an experienced, reliable guide to take you, you can find yourself lost for ever, swallowed up by the uncharted chasms of time and space.

The rabbi hooked his arm into my father's and led him to the pit filled with the corpses of those who had been killed that day. 'We are not in the world; the world is in us. Hold on tight to my belt. Close your eyes. Now we shall jump!' My father grabbed the end of the rabbi's coat and closed his eyes. When he opened them again he found that they were in a magical landscape that was difficult to describe because it was unlike anything known to humankind. According to the rabbi's testimony, standing before them was a mountain, exactly as described by Ansky in the play *The Dybbuk, or Between Two Worlds*: 'A high mountain, and on that mountain there is a huge rock, and from that huge rock a pure spring comes gushing out . . .' At the same time there was the sound of a beating heart, strong and deep, exactly as described by the famous playwright, 'because everything in the world has a heart and the world itself has one very large heart . . .' That is how the Hassidic rabbi of Bluzhov, quoting Shloyme Zanvi Rappoport (that being Ansky's full name), described what it was like after they had eradicated their own selves. Later, many years later, writes the rabbi, he discovered on one of his earthly voyages that there was just such a mountain and spring near the town of Lizhensk. The mountain was densely covered with woods, and the top of the rock overlooked a deep abyss. A strange sound rose from its depths, like the deep beating of a human heart. To this day they call the peak of that rock Rabbi Melech's Table.

What happened to my father? Rabbi Yisroel Spira had no answer to that question. They had not wanted to part, but the winds of time carried them off in different directions. Rabbi Yisroel Spira found his way to our world, but my father may still be wandering the corridors and labyrinths of many criss-crossing worlds.

SIX

In which a mysterious event is described but nothing is explained. Everything is in doubt, including life itself

It was two o'clock in the afternoon when the telephone rang.

'Albert Weisz?'

Holding the telephone with one hand, I wiped the sweat off my brow with the other. The rasping, chilling voice had been calling for the past few nights, always at the same time.

'Yes, this is Weisz.'

'Bertie,' said the stranger. That's what my mother used to call me, but she has been gone for a long time now.

'Who is that? Tell me. What do you want?'

No answer. The person at the other end of the telephone was silent. And then he hung up, as he always did when questioned.

Who is it that keeps disturbing me at night? Where is he calling from and why? I could not picture a face to go with that voice. Who is it behind that cold, metallic voice that has something unhuman about it? Maybe it is a voice straight from the grave. Why not? Technology is so advanced these days that anything is possible. Whoever is calling is certainly doing so for a reason. Does he suffer from insomnia like I do? But that is no explanation. It would be insane to think that these late-night calls have no purpose. Of course, that, too, is possible. The world is full of lunatics, and disturbed people are guided by their own mad ideas.

Such troubling thoughts give me insomnia. I amble around like a sleepwalker, put the water on for coffee, and as I wait for it to boil I step over to the window and peek out through the curtains at the deserted street. For a long time now I've had the feeling that I am being followed. And there, in the doorway of the building across the way, I spot the spy. He is hiding but his shadow gives him away. Who is he working for? Maybe he belongs to a secret neo-Nazi organization? Insufficient evidence for the police: just as it is impossible to place that rasping voice on the telephone, although its owner is obviously calling for some reason, so this spy is momentarily merely a shadow, or, rather, the shadow of a shadow, invisible yet present. I reported it to the nearby police station, and they wrote it up, but the good gentlemen did not take my complaint seriously. The police receive complaints of this nature every day from people of a certain age prone to fantasizing.

All the same, I found my visit to the police station and their lack of concern upsetting. I came out barely holding back my tears. I was deeply, truly humiliated that the police officer did not believe me. I've been enduring humiliation on a daily basis for a long time now.

I was not supposed to have survived. That's the problem. It was not planned for me to survive. I often talked about it with Solomon. We were connected by age and fate. Scientists had announced the discovery of a new particle, known as the God particle. The exciting findings of a decades'-long 'hunt' for a particle that could help humankind understand the birth of the universe were announced at a press conference, and they attracted a lot of international attention. But both Solomon and I, each in our own way, had been searching for the God particle that explained evil.

Solomon Levy was one of my few surviving friends. He's gone now, too. His death was a warning. But who cared about that? The papers merely carried a small, barely noticeable item saying that a senile old man had caused a fire in his flat, probably out of negligence, and that the place had been full of old papers and books. He alone was to blame for having been burned alive and enduring such a terrible death. The on-the-scene reporter wrote that the spacious three-room attic apartment was an absolute dump, crammed from floor to ceiling with old newspapers that the old man had collected, probably with the intention of selling them, so, when a cigarette end or cigar fell on them, it started a fire of catastrophic proportions. So many falsehoods in just a few lines of reporting. Solomon Levy did not smoke; anyone who knew him knew that, and the 'old papers' that the reporter describes were an important, indeed the most important part of his life's work: his collection of writings about the many forms of evil, from the Holocaust to the daily chronicles of crime. My late friend Solomon Levy could be described as a researcher. He was a diligent, devoted archivist of everything published on the subject of evil. He was collecting material for a comprehensive book he wanted to write about the criminal aggression that lies behind a wide range of behaviours, about different manifestations of wrongdoing and madness. I helped him to collect and classify this material. We met every day, trying to identify patterns that would give us a lead. It was our obsession, you might say. Day after day, crimes occurred that were so monstrous they defied the imagination:

Son kills sleeping father. Newborn baby drowned by mother and dumped on rubbish tip. Man sets vicious dog on neighbour and tosses corpse in well. Ninety-year-old woman raped by drunkard. Entire family murdered in moment of madness. Violent clashes between fifteen-year-old boys. Pathologically disturbed people organize fights between boys that they treat like dogs. Young man confesses he just killed a man and drank his blood. Killer paid by a local drug cartel and terrorizing Mexico is only twelve but has already murdered dozens of people. Polish woman stabs seven-year-old son and five-year-old daughter more than 150 times 'because there is evil in them'.

Over a period of just a few days there were lots of news items like that. No wonder Solomon was buried deep in newspaper clippings and articles. All these routine yet bizarre cases will be properly interpreted and explained once we find a mathematically reliable way to identify what they all have in common, what lies at the heart of such incidents; once we discover the actual 'seed of evil', the God particle we are looking for.

In the margin of an article about war crimes, my dear Solomon had quoted a poet who said that since time immemorial 'killers of all nationalities have belonged to but one nation, the nation of killers' and that 'everywhere the children of light and the children of darkness have already separated'.

A few days after the fire and Solomon Levy's funeral at the Jewish cemetery, I decided to go to the apartment of my deceased friend. I had the keys to his place just as he had to mine. We had both been on our own and had agreed to help one another if necessary.

But even with that key I could not help Solomon Levy any more.

Like a thief, which is what I was, I practically tiptoed up to Solomon's attic. The police had put up a No Entry sign. The stench of burning pervaded the corridor. Traces of the fire were everywhere.

I had an irresistible urge to see my friend's flat one last time; we had spent so many long hours talking there, having conversations that were very important to us. But the flat no longer belonged to Solomon, and I was afraid that I might be stopped and asked what I was doing there. Having barely managed to unlock the crooked wooden door, I stepped into a room that was unrecognizable. All you could see were the blackened, sooty rafters and charred pieces of furniture strewn around. Nothing worth mentioning was left, just the remains of a place where someone had once lived, traces of someone's life. Miraculously, a stack of papers written in Solomon's hand had survived. The flames had devoured everything but not this one pile of paper. I remembered the famous saying that manuscripts do not burn. Was it the Devil who said that or somebody close to him? Anyway, that was all that remained of our friendship. I had the right to take what had escaped the flames. But the moment I touched the sheets of paper they disintegrated into powder and ash. If these writings had ever held the unsolved secret of the origin of evil, that secret was now destroyed, and all our hopes and efforts to trace it were lost.

I hurried away from the place where my friend had so tragically died. I could not shake the uneasy feeling that an all-seeing eye was constantly watching me. Did it belong to the person who hounded me late at night; was that the reason for my long, troubling hours of insomnia?

Night was falling. The city lights went on. Everything now had its shadow: the trees, the houses, the few passers-by. My own shadow followed me, fear followed me; something in the darkness said, 'You can run, but you cannot escape!'

SEVEN

'A Storm of Murk'

Another one of 'ours' has gone. Who are 'ours'? The last of the righteous. The righteous hold this world together so that it does not fall apart. Solomon Levy, Misha Wolf, Uriel Cohen and me, Albert Weisz, the writer of this diary. The number four holds the world. Four is an important number. Solomon himself talked about the importance of the number four. There are four letters in God's name, four corners of the world, four seasons . . . He had read somewhere that in Japanese the word *shi* means both four and death and that the Japanese take great care not to say it aloud. He had developed a whole story around it, one worthy of Chesterton's Father Brown. A number that connects all of us but whose secret, hidden meaning harbours death itself. Was it an omen, a premonition or simply a coincidence? Misha Wolf does not accept coincidences. 'Everything is connected', he says, 'in time and in space. All destinies are part of a great web. All are in one and one is in all.'

Solomon had been feeling very poorly of late. Something had shocked him, something he had unexpectedly learned, I thought, but he doggedly refused to talk about it. Something was plaguing him. But who among our last generation of survivors hadn't been plagued by troubling thoughts and bad dreams? I had my own nightmares, my own continuous, obsessive dream, but I kept it to myself as something that was my problem and mine alone.

No, I have no explanation for Solomon's increasingly morose mood. Admittedly, there were a few incidents that I did not pay much attention to but that had left him visibly shaken. One morning somebody had sprayed a strange symbol on the front door of his building, a symbol I had never seen before. I would have ignored it had I not seen how badly it affected Solomon. He muttered something about 'primordial evil'. He did not answer my questions, just waved them away. I remembered all this later, after Solomon's funeral at the Jewish cemetery. I visited his grave to show him that even in death he was not alone and noticed that somebody had carefully chosen evenly shaped pieces of white quartz to form that very same symbol.

I leaf through my diary where I sometimes jot down my dilemmas, my fears, the hours when my loneliness is like a physical pain . . . All those deaths, what was the point if they ultimately proved to be meaningless? Ever since I can remember, ever since becoming a conscious being, I've been plagued by a feeling of guilt that I let down my father and mother, who were taken away to die a terrible death in the camps. I had promised to take care of my younger brother Elijah but had failed to save him. So why was I the one to survive? How can one believe in anything, in religion, in people, if every explanation loses all meaning?

Revenge came the following night when I sweated my way through a dream that I was standing in front of a firing squad. I could not see the soldiers' faces properly, their uniforms had only the odd Nazi detail, and they were preparing to carry out their task. The order is given, they raise their rifles, there is a moment of terrible tension and silence . . . and then . . . I wake up, look blankly at the play of shadows on the ceiling, my eyes involuntarily close again and I have the same dream that keeps repeating itself like a tape loop until morning.

Those nightmares were the reason I visited Emil Neifeld, an honorary member of the International Association of Psycho-analysts. He belongs to the oldest generation of survivors. He does not like to talk about himself or his family's past. He says he is an atheist, even though, he will add, atheists do not really exist. He has simply lost his faith. At the same time he is proud to be a loyal disciple of Sigmund Freud. Freud had also stressed his atheism; however, his discovery of the subconscious, the secret reading of the human soul, was based, Freud would admit when in a good mood, on the teachings of the old Kabbalah about the multi-layered text. The first reading, that first layer of the text, conceals the other layers, the true, complex interpretations. This simple explanation about the strong connection between science and mysticism is more than obvious. Hence, we can say that old Emil is an atheist who has rejected the mystical Kabbalah but applies its teachings.

Whenever I came to see Emil I usually found him comfortably ensconced in an old-fashioned armchair, part of the family's lost-and-found furniture, as he once told me. Things, like people, often have their own interesting, even tragic, stories to tell. Emil Neifeld had theories about everything, about the beginning and the end of the world, the meaning of fate, complex gender relations, the possibility of final cognition, and even how to cure colds and rheumatism. He spoke least about depression because, as he once put it, it is pointless to talk about mental disorders since they are largely organic in origin. Depression and melancholia, he maintained, are the sisters of euphoria and excessive optimism, and it is a well-known fact that extreme opposites have a common touching point. Human life unfolds between these two emotions, and the whole of human culture, of civilization, is derived from the clash between these extremes.

I liked visiting the old man precisely because he had simple explanations for everything.

'What you are now and the role that you play go back to your childhood, and you must make your peace with that fact. I advise all my friends to accept their illnesses as something that is a part of them, an integral part of their character, their mentality, their physical make-up and, to put it simply, their fate, and so they should make friends with these alleged "illnesses" and live with them sensibly, in true coexistence.'

Emil Neifeld sometimes looked like an old clown. His sagging cheeks were powdered, his nose was big and seemed to be artificially planted in the middle of his face and his eyes were light and a bit sad. Who was the old clown mocking? Nobody, just life itself.

He was not particularly surprised to hear that Solomon Levy had died. If you want to time your own death you have to be sensible, composed and, above all, self-disciplined. Giving up your own life is not in itself an act of cowardice or pessimism. Solomon Levy was a man with a secret. Recently he had experienced moments of deep depression, the kind that destroys you inside, the terrible 'storm of murk' that makes you ready to take your own life. It takes real courage to know when the time has come to accept your inexorable end with dignity and to embrace death voluntarily. It is an act that renounces life, the world and oneself. It is a decision that everyone has to make for himself, just as voluntary death, death by one's own hand, is something profoundly personal. 'Man can bear up under sufferings, but it is difficult for a man to endure the meaninglessness of suffering,' writes the Russian Berdyaev. 'The psychology of suicide is the psychology of man locked up in the isolation of himself.' It is to enter dark recesses from which one sees no way out.

For the Greeks, Romans and peoples of the East, suicide, in certain circumstances, is an act worthy of exceptional respect. Nowhere does the Talmud explicitly forbid suicide. The famous mass suicide of those who chose to defend Masada rather than be enslaved, the Zealots' desperate self-immolation when they threw themselves into the fire after the second destruction of the Temple and the mass suicide in York some ten centuries later to avoid forced conversion have been celebrated and honoured throughout history, and these people were proclaimed holy martyrs even though post-Talmudists, along with Christian authorities, maintained that suicide is a sin greater than murder because it rejects the doctrine of reward and punishment in the next world and undermines the sanctity of God.

The act our friend Solomon Levy committed, on this I agreed with old man Neifeld, was one of being true to himself and to his courage. He spurned a life that was losing all meaning. At the very end, in his last conscious moment, he must have felt that he had no other choice than to do what he did.

Still, if I could, I would love to ask him whether there really was no other choice.

NEWS

Ana Ferria Santos gave birth to a boy who started walking at just four weeks old, who makes terrifying cackling sounds and breathes fire

BOGOTÁ:
A REAL HORROR

Ana Ferria Santos (28) from the Colombian town of Lorica, near the Caribbean coast, gave birth to a demon-baby who started walking when only four weeks old, who makes terrifying cackling noises and is capable of breathing fire. She says that her joy at the birth of her son very quickly turned into terrible fear because after a while she suspected that the child was the Antichrist in disguise.

The appearance and behaviour of Ana's baby struck terror in the hearts of the whole family. The little boy soon got out of bed and started moving around and hiding in the house. He likes to jump out of his hiding place and terrify everybody with his menacing eyes and terrible voice.

'He walks like an adult, sometimes going off and hiding under the bed, in a suitcase, in the washing machine or in the fridge, as if deliberately trying to scare me. I can't control him,' said the miserable Ana, speaking on Colombian radio.

Her neighbours are afraid for their own safety because they claim that the child is possessed by the Devil, which is why he is able to breathe fire.

'I saw burn marks on his clothes, and we heard that they were also found where he usually sits. The fire he breathes has burned the palms of his hands,' said a frightened neighbour.

Afraid that the Antichrist in their neighbourhood would harm them and their families, her neighbours repeatedly attacked Ana and her husband Oscar Palencia López, stoned their house and tried to make them leave Lorica and take their demon child as far away as possible.

Doctors Launch an Investigation

The Colombian police and Catholic Church have refused to accept that black magic has entered the soul of Ana Santos's and Oscar López's infant, but doctors have decided to study the child. A team composed of a psychologist, social workers, a nutritionist and a lawyer will also look into this unusual case, and they have already said that the child has shown signs of being possessed by the Devil.

EIGHT

In which we learn how evil inhabits human beings,
even though it is not of human origin

'What creature is this inside me, what monster, and whence does
it come?'

St Augustine

I often talked with Misha Wolf about demonology and the impact
of external forces on human behaviour. He is utterly contemptuous
of the other world. I try to convince him, to no avail, that if we
want to explain a phenomenon in psychiatry or psychopathology
we have to set aside traditional interpretations and look at areas
which science and psychiatry have hitherto considered taboo. I
do not hesitate to talk to priests about mystical elements in the
Christian, Muslim and Jewish faiths. Mysticism is merely the
deepening of faith. There have been mystics in the past, and there
still are today, who have healed and cured people of the effects of
the very worst traumas and mental disorders. Of course, you have
to beware of charlatans; there are many, and they can be found
everywhere. I asked Misha to join me on a visit. Because of the
unusual nature of this visit I am writing down the salient points.

I had already heard of the case; it had even been written up, in
a sensationalist way, needless to say. It concerned a boy who was
five but looked like an old man.

I examined the boy's medical papers. They said that he suffered from 'seriously underactive thyroid glands. Because of this hypo-thyroidism his physical development was stunted, but mentally he showed signs of an extraordinary memory, unquestionable intelligence and yet a lack of any real communication skills or socialization'.

M.N. and his son live in a modest house by the Danube, but they are not poor. The child is said to be a 'boy wonder', clairvoyant, with prophetic powers. The father knows how to exploit this and charges a fee to meet and talk to the five-year-old. The boy's speech is a strange mixture – he mutters, utters unintelligible words and emits shrieks that sound more animal-like than human, and M.N. translates what the boy has 'said'. The neighbours are terrified of the little monster. One of them reported the case to the police. Two policemen came on an official call. I saw their report. They were unable to evaluate properly what they saw and left it up to the Church and the doctors to deal with the case. Obviously, they were both fascinated and frightened by the child. They called it 'the Devil's work' and there the matter ended.

M.N. agreed to meet us under certain conditions. He requested that we both pay his fee and that it remain between us. I agreed to his terms, and the meeting took place as described below.

Subject: Demon Child
Date: Tuesday 17 July 2012; 15.37

'I always wanted a son. My Ana didn't care if we had a boy or a girl. There was no end to our joy when we learned that we were about to become parents

'We talked to him while he was still in Ana's tummy. Ana heard his voice the first time she felt him move. I put my ear against her tummy and heard it, too. It was an adult's voice – rough, rasping – which seemed strange, but this was our child, and whatever was a part of him was a part of us as well. It did not frighten us.

'What did we talk about? Actually, he did all the talking, although we barely understood a thing he said. He mentioned places we had no idea existed, weird, strange, foreign names. We just wondered how an unborn child could know all these things and who had taught him, because we certainly hadn't.

'My Ana died in childbirth. He took her life. I'm certain that was the price of his birth.

'From day one he looked different from the other children. He had the face, sunken eyes and skull of an old man. Like a child-grandpa.

'He liked to hide and then jump out and terrify everybody with his demonic eyes and terrible voice.

'You can talk to him now.'

Antonio's story, as translated by M.N.

'I do not know how I wound up imprisoned in a human body. Somebody threw me in, and there I was. But not alone. The embryo of a small living creature was there as well, almost shapeless at first, but then it started assuming a human form. I took advantage of the little creature and slipped into its body.

'There was no way for me to tell anybody how different the two of us were and that we could not survive side by side. I am very old, and he had only just come into this world. The trouble was that the only way I could communicate with the outside world was through him. Essentially I am not human; mine is an entirely different kind of existence, multi-layered, superior, unpredictable.

I repulse people because it is hard for them to comprehend and accept my existence. I devoured my little double, overpowered him and destroyed him. Once I acquired his voice he became superfluous. I discarded him like a shell.

'The human body I carry is not the real me; at first I only sensed it, but later I was sure. Gifted with foresight, I often imagined a strange, serpent-like figure whispering to me what I really looked like. Finally, I managed to see with my inner eye exactly who I am. I saw myself, the mythical *catoblepas*, curled up at the bottom of its human hideaway, a self-devouring creature with gaping jaws whose breath can turn people into stone or kill them. I take the form of the person I have killed. I am and am not the boy, you see. The devouring that has begun inside will last until I swallow the very last morsel of my own self. Until I turn, in both spirit and body, into nothingness. And nothingness is the primeval beginning of everything.'

M.N., his eyes at half-mast as if hypnotized, translated Antonio's confused words; he spoke quickly, fluently, without hesitation, as if the story was not new to him. Every so often the boy's mutterings became shrieks that were almost unbearable for the human ear to hear. M.N. would calm the boy down, gently stroking his bald head.

When the tirade was over, we moved to the second part of the visit.

I asked about Elijah. According to his father, Antonio was able to see the future as well as the past, so could he tell me what happened to my little brother? M.N. gave me a startled look. I hadn't told him what I was going to ask this supposedly all-seeing creature. But when I placed two large bills in his hand, he composed himself and repeated my question in a language that only he and the boy understood.

Instead of an answer, any answer, Antonio started rocking from side to side, white foam appeared on his lips and he put his little hands up to his ugly old face.

And then the little creature, I don't know what else to call him, stood up and, swaying to some strange rhythm on thin little legs that barely held him up, screamed, and to our amazement started clearly calling out various names, presumably the names of some demons from the East.

'Gallu, Maskim, Ishtar, Typhon, Asmodeus, Azazel, Behemoth, Leviathan, Samael, Lilith, Iblis . . .'

Laughing in the rasping voice of a man, the tiny little body twirled to a rhythmic tune that only he could hear. His father, let us call him that, sat in a corner of the room, following the boy's movements, barely moving his lips. This repeated enumeration of names was the answer, the utterly meaningless answer. Then suddenly the boy went quiet and rigid; only the colour of the ugly boy-grandpa's eyes changed. They turned green and gleamed with a malevolent light.

'In the pale, cold moonlight a pale, translucent boy is riding a white horse with the head of a dog . . . the little horseman is gripped with fear and panic, alone on the back of an animal that he is not steering and that is taking him who knows where.'

Misha Wolf had lost patience. Even during the session he had been shaking his head, scowling, fidgeting, taking off his glasses and wiping them with the chamois leather he carried around in his wallet.

But now he thought that things had gone too far. He turned to M.N. 'You can't fool me. I know the trick of talking from your diaphragm. When I was a boy I was fascinated by it. But I'm not a child any more. Nor is this gentleman here beside me. I watched your boy. He's got a rare disorder called progeria. It accelerates the aging process. It's cruel of you to exploit the boy's tragic condition. I wonder if you're even his father. You are taking advantage of his desperate condition to make money out of his illness. Talking from the diaphragm is a cheap trick, sir.'

M.N. did not immediately reply. He turned red in the face, his eyes burned, he seethed and then suddenly exploded. 'You don't believe it! You don't believe it! What are you saying, that my son and I are common crooks?' He turned to the boy, who had nodded off and was only half awake, still rocking from side to side. 'Hear that, son? He doesn't believe us!'

He clapped his hands. The boy screamed so loudly I had to cover my ears. The door to the next room opened, and a swarm of insects came pouring out, crawling and flying around us, making strange sounds, followed by an onslaught of rats and lizards and snakes and all sorts of other creepy, slithery creatures.

It was a cacophony of shrieks, screams and cries. Misha Wolf pulled at my sleeve.

'Let's get out of here. Now!'

And we ran out of the house without looking back. When we were sufficiently far away, we sat down on a bench by the river to catch our breath.

'You see what suggestion and hypnosis can do?' Misha Wolf said, wiping the sweat off his brow. 'That old goat knows lots of tricks. First, talking from the diaphragm and then the hypnosis.'

'You really think there was nothing of the Devil there?' I asked.

'Nothing, honestly, believe me,' he said, dismissively waving his hand. 'All gimmicks, just gimmicks. It's easy to trick people.

There are so many manias, my friend. There's cartacoethes, doromania, gamomania, onomatomania, clinomania, enosimania, trichotillomania, aboulomania . . . Do you want to know what they mean?' Misha asked. I motioned no.

'The one we witnessed,' Misha continued, ignoring my gesture, 'is demonomania, the belief that somebody is possessed by the Devil. I must admit, the child looks terrifying, but he's just a child who has been punished by nature, whereas that man who says he is his father is a dangerous charlatan,' he said, scowling. 'I watched you the whole time. I have the feeling that you were terrified. You believed it, didn't you?'

We sat on the bench a little longer and then headed for town. Every few steps I looked back to see if we were being followed.

Out of all the things Misha Wolf said, only two words stuck in my mind: 'old goat'. Had it been just a slip of the tongue, or had he deliberately used those specific words for M.N.? Everybody knows that is what people mockingly call the Prince of Darkness.

NINE

*The gathering in New York; the stories
of lost and abandoned children*

Yes, 'the storm of murk'. A dangerous state of depression. Let us
go back a number of years to when Albert Weisz, Uriel Cohen
and Professor Misha Wolf first met. Along with about a dozen
other passengers from Yugoslavia they arrived at New York's
LaGuardia Airport. Members of the American Jewish community
who had organized the international conference welcomed them.
On Saturday the Marriot Hotel, where they were staying, was
hosting The First International Gathering of Children Hidden
During the Second World War, bringing together people who
had grown up under false names and been saved under unusual
circumstances. It was attended by about two thousand people,
most of whom, it was reported, were fifty-somethings. Their stories
were sad, often incredible, and their rescue was like a miracle. A
girl from Poland recounted how her mother had thrown her off
the Poniatowski Bridge into the Vistula River when they were
being taken to a Nazi concentration camp. Some good people had
pulled her out of the water, other good people had taken her in
and raised her, and she never saw her mother again. Another girl

told how her mother had wrapped her in a blanket and left her on the pavement.

'I lay there for three days. Nobody dared to pick me up because they knew I was Jewish. A German police officer fed me. He brought me a bottle of milk several times a day, telling people that he couldn't kill me because he had a two-month old baby of his own at home. Finally, a good woman picked me up and hid me in her village.

There was story after story of this nature. Everyone at the conference had his or her own tale to tell. Some people wept as they spoke, others wept as they listened.

One woman said, 'Some good people took me from the hospital in Garwolin. They knew I was a Jewish child that somebody had left there. They never found out who it was. I never learned the name of my mother or father.'

Michelle from France sobbed as she recounted how her parents had hidden her in the basement during a raid and told her not to make a sound. She spent two days and two nights like that until the neighbours found her and took her away to a village. She survived, but she remembers her parents' faces only vaguely because she was just three at the time.

Next it was the turn of the lost, abandoned, forgotten children from Yugoslavia.

'I am Esther Shapiro. My parents met and married in 1940, and I was born in April 1941. The people from the Red Cross saw that my mother was about to give birth and managed to pull her out of the column of Jews and get her to a hospital to have her baby. Her entire family was sent to Auschwitz. My mother had her baby and hid in the hospital for five months, but then somebody betrayed her. My mother had met a nurse her age and had said to her, "If anything happens to me, please take my child and save her." When my mother was denounced and taken away as a Jew, the young nurse took me home with her. My true identity had to be kept from the neighbours and the other children. So I grew up under a false name and false identity. It was not until I started school and the war had long been over that my foster mother told me who I was. I found it hard to accept. I was shocked. I felt cheated. I wanted to kill myself, to disappear. Yes, I felt doubly cheated, by my real parents and by my foster mother.

Maria Demayo took the floor.

'My mother was at home with me and my sister. A police officer came with orders to take her away. My mother started packing the bare essentials. The police officer couldn't help saying, "Don't you know where they are taking you? At least hide the children. That way they've got a chance of surviving; maybe the neighbours will take them in." My mother quickly came to a decision: she left the apartment and the two of us behind. I was two and my sister four . . .'

'My name is Sonia. I wasn't registered as a Jew because I was baptized as a Serb at St Alexander Nevsky Church. Two of Belgrade's worst, most notorious policemen, Kosmajac and Banjac, came for my mother. Why didn't they take me with her? I was sickly from the day I was born. I suffered from malnutrition because we were poor after they hanged my father. I got rickets and stopped walking. When they came to take my mother away, our neighbour Maria asked Kosmajac if she could keep the child. He glanced at me, laughed and said, "You call *that* a child? She'll die on us in the barracks; with you she'll live another week. Why take her?" And that's how I survived. I was two at the time. Before she was taken away, my mother said to Auntie Maria, "I've got just three requests: braid her hair, don't give her a sewing needle because sewing didn't help feed either of us and don't teach her to pray because today is the Epiphany and it is this day that they've chosen to take me away from my child." And they led her away. She didn't even kiss me goodbye. I'm so sorry that I don't have a photograph of my mother and father.'

Albert Weisz spoke about his despair at losing his little brother. When they learned that they were being taken to a camp, their parents had managed to throw them both off the train. Albert looked everywhere for his little brother. It was night, bone-chillingly cold, and he searched and searched until he almost dropped, but there was neither hide nor hair of little Elijah. Tears streamed down his face as he spoke at the conference in the Marriot Hotel. He went on to talk about the *Volksdeutsche* forest ranger who had found him and taken him home with him. Then he recounted how he had run away. Where could a seven-year-old boy run to? There was an island in the middle of the river; they called it the Island of the Dead. Villagers would bring their sick animals there to die or dump their carcasses there. Young Albert had no real concept of the word 'death'. Was it something permanent, or was it temporary? How did it happen and why? It seemed perfectly reasonable, at least to a seven-year-old, to take himself there. Johann and Ingrid, the forest ranger and his wife, always spoke of the Island of the Dead as a place inhabited by the souls of the disappeared or dead.

'I spent three days and three nights on the island. That was when I really grew up. Among the carcasses of the animals. Some were already skeletons; others were still decomposing. That's when I learned that dying is like disintegrating, disappearing, perhaps for ever, that it was different from the kind of temporary disappearance my father had attempted as a sort of hiding game, different from trying to make yourself invisible. When night fell I was scared. Scared of the impenetrable darkness and the voices I heard. Perhaps I only imagined the voices, but, then again, perhaps I didn't. Who knows what happens in the heart of darkness? It was even worse when the full moon peeked out from behind the cloud. I was a child, and my imagination could not distinguish between mere shadows and the emanations of some other, strange, mysterious world. I still carry some of that fear inside me.'

On the third night Albert felt a touch on his shoulder. His eyes shot open, and he saw something like a fleecy cloud, a shape that somehow reminded him of his father. The voice was a bit hoarse, but it was unquestionably his father's.

His father told him that magic had led him astray into another world and that the only way he found to leave it was as a spirit, a shadow, a wisp of fog. But he said he had not lost hope, and Albert shouldn't either. If there was a way in then there was a way out, and he would find it. That is what the wisp of fog that was Albert's father told him.

Albert continued. "'Father, where is Elijah?" I asked. "We got separated. How can I find my little brother? He's still very small and can't take care of himself." "You're right," said my father's shadow. "He's too small to take care of himself. But, wherever you are, he is always there. He goes where you go. He has taken the shape of a bird, my boy. Look up." And sure enough, I spotted a colourful little bird up in the tree. It fluttered its wings and flew around my head. It was him, my little brother!'

Albert had barely finished his story when there was a commotion in the auditorium. A colourful little bird had come from who knows where and was flying above Albert's head. Somebody had the presence of mind to open all the windows, and the little bird, startled by the noise, circled the auditorium one last time before flying away.

TEN

When day breaks; Misha Wolf's story

Next it was the turn of a tall, grey-haired, seventy-year-old man to tell his story.

'Until two years ago I thought I knew everything there was to know about my origins, my parents. I had a quiet childhood on a farm that seldom saw soldiers; I was doubly protected by my older brother and my hard-working parents. I vaguely remember those days and the old farmhouse where we lived. It was a happy, peaceful childhood. But two years ago, when they were digging up the ground to lay water pipes at Staro Sajmište, Belgrade's Old Fairground, which was once a concentration camp, the workers discovered a tin box, the kind in which they used to sell biscuits and sweets. A prisoner named Avram Wolf, who sensed that the end was near, had buried the box. It contained letters, photographs, documents and sheets of music he had composed in the camp. Found among the papers was a note:

Dearest Misha
Maybe you will never have to read this letter. Maybe all will end

well. But these are dangerous, uncertain times. So we want you to know how much we love you and that we can hardly wait for all of us to be together again. Mama can't stop crying, and I can't console her. The Brankovs, who are taking care of you, are our friends, and they will be good to you and treat you like their own son.

'Only then did I learn who my real parents were. By pure chance.'
Misha Wolf opened his violin case, which he had been holding under his arm.

'This is the music that my father started composing in the camp and that I finished. I think he deliberately left it unfinished as a way for me to connect with him.'

He played the piece with its interweaving klezmer, kaddish and Lekhah Dodi motifs. His father's composition sounded like an ode to life in the face of death. The old musician played his heart out. Everyone in the audience wept; they were listening to a voice from the other side, and the old musician wept, too.

What else can be said about the violinist Misha Wolf's story? That the discovery of the tin box radically changed his life. And when one's life and identity change at an age when life is nearing its end, it is like a tumultuous inner earthquake. Truth be told, Misha's first reaction was not to open the box, but, when he did, he tumbled into an abyss of time. Everything seemed a lie, both what he believed to be true and what really was true.

As the pretty blonde curator of the Jewish Historical Museum held out the box of documents from the Sajmište, he wondered for a second if he should even take it because he was certain that it must be some sort of misunderstanding.

'Where did you get the idea that I have anything to do with that box?'

The woman waiting for him to take the box answered his question with another question. 'You *are* Misha Brankov?' she asked.

'Yes, I am Misha Brankov.'

The woman shrugged her shoulders. 'A note found with these papers says that if Avram and Ilda do not leave the camp alive, this box and its contents should be handed over to the Brankov family that had taken in their two-year-old son Misha.'

'Oh, come on!' the professor said, waving her away as if to fend her off.

The curator continued, 'Before we phoned to notify you, we spoke to a close friend of the Wolf family . . . Emil Neifeld. He confirmed that Ilda and Avram Wolf left their two-year old boy in the care of the Brankov family.'

'That's impossible. Impossible,' the music professor muttered. 'Give me the address of this gentleman . . . what did you say . . . Nei . . . Neifeld.' He took the box from the curator while she jotted down Neifeld's address on a piece of paper.

The professor walked through the park carrying the tin box. He stopped at an unoccupied bench and sat down. He looked around. Some dogs were tearing around in the park while their owners chatted. Two young men and a girl were sitting at the foot of the monument drinking beer out of two-litre plastic bottles. Children were swinging on excruciatingly squeaky swings . . . The professor placed the box on his lap and put his hands over it. He felt its metal touch under his fingers.

*

Neifeld was waiting for him in front of his apartment door. He was old, very old, his hair grey, his eyebrows white. He found it an effort to walk. He lived alone.

'I'm the only one of my generation left. I'm the last living witness,' he said.

They sat down in the living-room, and through the glass door he could see an unmade bed; another door led to the kitchen. The professor placed his tin box on the table.

'They gave me this box at the museum and told me an incredible story.'

Neifeld nodded. 'Yes, I heard. What's so incredible about it?'

'The box and its contents supposedly belonged to my real parents. That's so absurd . . . I don't know how to put it . . .'

'It's not a story, my dear man. I knew both families, the Wolfs and the Brankovs. The Brankovs had a farm where we all used to gather – the Weisz family, Isaac and Sara, and their sons Albert and Elijah, who had only just started walking. The cutest little thing I ever saw. Avram, your father, played several instruments, as I recall . . . He was a gifted musician. And your mother Ilda, she was a real beauty. We were all a bit in love with her. Your father . . . You said you are in the music world?'

Misha nodded.

'Well, there you are. It's in the genes. The Brankovs had a son, Kosta . . .'

'Kosta? You're sure that was his name?'

'Yes, he was called Kosta.' Neifeld struggled to his feet and shuffled into the kitchen. He returned with a tray bearing two cups of coffee. 'The occupation changed our lives completely. Race laws, yellow armbands. Still, we thought it was all temporary. Lots of terrible things happened. It's dangerous to dig into the past. Painful.'

Misha took the cup of coffee and was silent for a moment.

'So you are convinced that I am Misha Wolf?'

Old Neifeld nodded. 'You can't imagine what parents did to save their children. They wrapped them in blankets, left them at people's doors, begged strangers on the street to take them. Still, you were lucky. Very few people had any idea of the terrible times that lay ahead. I did. After Belgrade was bombed and the Germans came, my father was sent to work on the forced-labour gangs clearing away the rubble. With the help of friends I managed to obtain an *Ausweis* for my father, mother, the Wolfs and me to get out. I begged, I implored them to leave, but they wouldn't. But your father Avram managed to hide you with friends in the countryside, 'until things blow over', as he put it. I hesitated about leaving my parents and Belgrade. My parents died in the Semlin Judenlager concentration camp. In December 1941 the German occupying authorities decided to establish the camp on the site of the Old Fairground in what is today New Belgrade. It was a concentration camp for Roma and Jews. The people of Belgrade could see the women and children being transported from the centre of town to the big pavilions at the fairground. As bitter winter set in, more and more exhausted inmates died, and every few days you could see Jews from the camp pulling the dead across the frozen Sava River and handing them over to the Belgrade authorities for burial. In March 1942 it was decided to close the camp and finish off the inmates. I hid for a long time at a friend's place. By the time I decided to make a run for it, it was too late. I was arrested at the railway station. The Serbian Special Police had set a trap. An informer from our district named Ruben Rubenovich recognized me and pointed me out to the police. That's how I wound up being sent to Auschwitz.'

*

After several hours on the bus and then on foot through fields of yellow sunflowers, Misha stood in front of the big wooden door. It creaked as he pushed it open. In the courtyard were the granary, barn and tool shed – all ravaged by time and dilapidated – and a chained dog that started barking. Misha had grown up here. Kosta and his wife Ana were delighted to see him. They sat down on the bench in front of the house, Ana served them quince brandy and when she went back into the house Misha asked his 'brother', 'Kosta, why did you never tell me?'

'Tell you what?' Kosta asked, surprised.

'That we're not brothers.'

Kosta bowed his head. He said nothing for a moment and then replied, 'Because you *are* my brother. You've always been my brother. From the moment Mum and Dad brought you to the farm and said, "Kosta, this is your brother," I embraced you as my brother.'

Misha simply shook his head. 'Do you think that's enough of an explanation?' His eyes welled up with tears.

The professor and Kosta were cycling down a country lane, dismounting whenever there was a steep incline or rut in the road. The winter sun was already receding towards the horizon, and clouds were gathering in the sky.

They cycled through the woods of locust trees and came out into a clearing. They stopped at the village cemetery with its dozen timeworn, badly damaged crosses and gravestones. The railing around the cemetery was dangling, broken, and most of the graves were overgrown with grass and brushwood. They left their bikes by the entrance.

Kosta walked ahead. He stopped in front of the gravestone and cleared away the weeds. There was an inscription, *Jovan Brankov 1908–1985*, and underneath it, *Vera Brankov 1912–1983*. Above was a porcelain photograph: Vera and Jovan when they were young.

Kosta pulled two candles out of his pocket. He handed one to the professor. They lit them and placed them at the base of the gravestone.

'Why didn't they tell me? It wasn't dangerous after the war, not for them or for me.'

'They couldn't imagine you being sent to an orphanage. They made me swear not to tell you. You didn't want for anything. They loved you, maybe even more than they loved me.'

The professor bowed his head. 'Still, wasn't it all just one big lie?'

'No, it wasn't. They loved you. Everything else may have been a lie but not that.'

Dark clouds blocked out the sun. Thunder rolled in the distance. The first drops of rain started falling. The two old men remained standing in front of the gravestone. Kosta took a step towards Misha and embraced him.

'Forgive, Misha.'

'What, Kosta? What am I supposed to forgive?'

'Well, everything, I guess. Forgive everything.'

The rain was coming down hard now. But the two men did not move.

The professor was in his room, sitting at his desk. In front of him was the open box. He took out a few old photographs: Avram Wolf conducting a chamber orchestra, a portrait of Avram's wife

Ilda, their wedding picture . . . His eye was drawn to a photograph of Avram and Ilda Wolf holding a little boy in her arms. The man and woman are smiling. The professor turned over the picture: *July 1941* was written on the back.

The professor passed his hand over the photograph as if trying to capture some of its magic.

He put the picture to one side, took the letter out of the box and read it.

Dearest Misha

Maybe you will never have to read this letter. Maybe all will end well. But these are dangerous, uncertain times. So we want you to know how much we love you and that we can hardly wait for all of us to be together again. Mama can't stop crying, and I can't comfort her.

Day and night a melody rings in my ears. It's a testimony to us. That we existed. I fall asleep and wake up to its strains. I have always believed that music is more powerful than anything, than all these horrors, than dying, than death even. And, in some way, I think that as long as this music lives, so will we.

The professor placed the letter on the table and took the handbound manuscript book from the box. Written on the cover were the words: WHEN DAY BREAKS, and underneath, in smaller letters:

> When day breaks
> And the dead awaken
> And a new dawn arrives
> And the night is gone

We shall be here
When day breaks
And the night is gone . . .

The professor leafed through the score. It was obviously unfinished. He drummed the beat on the desk with his fingers. He tried to hum the notes.

He stood up, walked over to the piano and played a few notes. Suddenly he stopped. He felt inordinately excited; he was connecting with his parents. He applied his fingers to the keyboard again, more decisively this time, picking out the tune from the damaged score, some of it legible, some of it completely missing. He tried to improvise but was not happy with it. He struck the keys, tentatively at first, and then with increasing confidence.

And so began the professor's obsession. He played his father's unfinished composition on the piano several times. The melody haunted him day and night. It reached out from the depths of the past. Through its coded musical language, his real father, Avram Wolf, had forged a connection with the future, with his absent son, by telling the tragic tale of those terrible times and sending a message that the professor had yet to fully comprehend. If he was to understand it, he first had to learn more about the secrets of Jewish music and complete the unfinished composition. True, he knew a little about synagogue music, that the songs sung in Sephardic synagogues were different from those sung in Ashkenazi synagogues; he had heard something about the folk music of the Ashkenazim, about klezmer music, the roots of which could be traced back to traditional Jewish music that, over time, had been influenced by the music of other peoples living in the region where Jews resided; he had once heard a concert of klezmer music in

Budapest and had been greatly impressed by the clarinettist and cellist. But what his father had composed, surrounded by barbed wire and people condemned to death, was something else. It sounded different; it was both familiar and unfamiliar. An unsolvable mystery seemed to face the professor. And obviously it was not just about the music. He decided to talk to the rabbi in Belgrade. The rabbi received him politely; he had heard about his story.

'We are a small community and word spreads quickly. What has happened is nothing short of a miracle. To learn the truth about your parents after such a long time and in such a way.'

He looked through the score that had been preserved in the tin box.

'You know what they say, Professor. Music is the soul of the universe. The heavens sing, the Throne of God radiates with music, even the tetragrammaton of Yahweh is composed of four musical notes. Every person is a song unto himself and can express himself through musical notes. Your father knew that.' The rabbi stopped for a moment. 'What is written here is indeed Hassidic music. Some people believe that the soul of the musician comes through Hassidic music. That you can hear your father's voice.'

And that is exactly what Misha heard. His father's voice. He returned home with the musical score of the Kabbalistic and Hassidic songs. Hassidism is connected to the Kabbalah and its mysticism. The Professor became increasingly convinced that the composition was a kind of prayer that enabled a heightened level of devotion, wherein the difference between past and present disappeared and the gates of time opened up.

He spent hours at the piano finishing his father's composition. He no longer knew if it was day or night, if he was awake or asleep;

a space was opening up for the living and the dead to meet.

One night the professor was awoken by the wail of a siren. He got up and looked out of his ground-floor-apartment window. The cobbled street and building opposite were bathed in moonlight. Soldiers toting submachine-guns were herding people out into the street. Women, children, the elderly, with their bundles and suitcases, filled the entire street. You could hear children crying and soldiers shouting '*Schnell! Schnell!* Hurry up!'

The professor ran out into the street. He noticed that everybody was wearing a yellow armband with the Star of David on it. He walked over to the line of people and asked what was going on, but he received no answer. Even the German soldier ignored him. He pushed his way to the head of the queue looking for his parents, Avram and Ilda Wolf. He spotted them, but every time he drew near them they somehow slipped out of his reach.

The Semlin Judenlager was silhouetted in the moonlight. In the middle of the camp was the tower with its sinister searchlight: a lighthouse in the dark. Streams of people poured into the jaws of the camp.

The professor tried to find his parents in the crowd, but the searchlight strafing the grounds blinded him. There was lots of noise: abandoned and lost children running around, a group of blind people holding on to one another, German Shepherds barking. It was utter pandemonium.

Rows of wooden, four-tier bunk beds stood in the open space. The elderly tried to climb on to them, fell off and tried again, holding on to the wooden frames.

There was the wail of a siren. An armoured truck, also known as a *Gaswagen*, or gas van, drove through the camp's open gates. It stopped in the middle of the grounds. Everyone fell silent. The back door of the truck silently opened. The inmates calmly stepped into the gaping dark hole of the vehicle. Out of nowhere a voice read out their names:

'Mandil Avram, Mandil Eva, Teichner Otto, Reis Artur, Cohen Esther, Levi Josif, Schwartz Geza, Calderon Mosha, Kalef Lenka, Avramović Rafailo, Nachmias Luna, Adanya Chaim, Melamed Mosha, Đurković Adela, Kalmić Isak, Semo Lazar, Amar Solomon, Demayo Jakov, Cohen Oscar, Beracha Josif, Finci Mosha, Weiner Ana, Singer Charlotta, Singer Greta . . .'

The list of names went on and on; the vehicle kept taking people in, as if it had unlimited space. The professor heard the names 'Ilda and Avram Wolf . . .' He saw his mother and father step into the truck. But first they turned around to look for him. He shouted as loud as he could, but no sound came out of his mouth.

The next day the professor set out on foot to the place where the Jewish camp once stood. He crossed Brankov Bridge and walked through a grassy field to the Old Fairground. Here, next to the dilapidated pavilions, stood a new crop of shanties housing refugees and Roma. Although tens of thousands of people died here, there was nothing to show that this had once been the site of a Jewish concentration camp and then a transit camp. He came to the place where workers laying new water pipes had recently discovered the box that had changed his life. There was earth in the ditch now, but you could still recognize the spot. The professor bowed and carefully placed a bouquet of flowers. He stood there quietly for a few seconds. Then he took his violin out of the case he had been carrying under his arm. He played 'When Day Breaks' the way his father, Avram Wolf, had written it, along with the part he,

Misha Wolf, Avram's son, had added. It was now a finished, complete melody; he had paid the debt owed to his father but also to all those who had gone from this place to their deaths.

ELEVEN

The House of Remembering and Forgetting

Albert could not sleep. This visit to New York and the stories he had heard there had upset him. He tossed and turned, but sleep was nowhere to be found. He glanced at his watch; it was already past midnight. He left his bed and walked over to the window. The tall building opposite blocked his view. His hotel room suddenly seemed tiny, stifling. He dressed quickly, took the elevator downstairs, walked past the reception desk and out into the crisp night air. The broad avenue, bordered by tall buildings that seemed to touch the nocturnal sky, was still busy with cars. Skyscrapers made Albert particularly uneasy and dizzy. He walked on, looking for a quieter part of this big city.

Eventually he came to an unfamiliar part of New York, and already he felt better. There was hardly a soul in the street and almost no cars. Albert thought that this part of New York looked better at night than in daytime. Some way back he had veered off the street his hotel was on, ignoring the conference organizers' warnings that parts of the city were dangerous at night and that they should stick to Manhattan. Clouds periodically obscured the full moon. Albert wanted to return to his hotel but was confused by the jumble of unfamiliar streets. The pleasure of taking a stroll gave way to panic.

He wandered around for a while and then on a corner noticed a neon sign and an open door. He hurried over, thinking that someone there might be able to help him. As he got closer, he saw that the sign said: *The House of Remembering and Forgetting.*

There was nobody inside. A screen glowed in the middle of the open space. Otherwise it was completely empty; there was only the screen. Its flickering light illuminated the bare walls.

A sign appeared on the screen: *The Remembering Room.*

Albert walked over to the screen. He typed two words on the keyboard: Weisz family. For a second the screen went blank, then there was a flickering of horizontal and vertical lines, and when the picture stabilized he saw his father and mother, his seven-year-old self and Elijah. They were walking in a column of people, his father carrying a suitcase, his mother pulling Elijah by the hand and he, Albert, keeping trying to keep pace with them. In front and behind were the distraught faces of women, children and the elderly. What mysterious photographer had immortalized this picture, one that Albert could not get out of his head? Albert Weisz was once again convinced of what he had always believed: nothing that happens ever disappears; one way or another, everything is forever recorded.

He saw himself trudging across a snowy field, he saw Johann and Ingrid, the Island of the Dead . . . The images flitted by, one after another, all familiar pictures that he had kept to himself and for himself. He saw himself passing through torched villages, hiding in the woods, being given food by people who took pity on the ragged boy, on this boy who did not answer questions, this lonely creature so full of hate, fear and despair. Then there he was in the orphanage with hundreds of other equally wild boys. Next came his escape from the bleak asylum and the railway tracks he followed in the hope of finding some trace of his parents. He watched the trains come and go. He saw himself growing up during these painfully hard years, he saw the orphanage where he had started talking again, first in stammers then in screaming rage, the wild boy, nobody's boy. The images flashed by, but Albert registered each and every one of them because this was his life. And, finally, he saw himself on the screen, in that powerful mirror, as an adult. He stood there alone, looking at the reflection of his own helplessness.

Remembering can bring great pain. Albert had been carrying this pain inside him for a long time, a pain that pervaded and filled his entire body, a pain that would not go away, that became ever-more present with each passing year.

Looking at the screen, Albert saw what he had seen so many times before, both in his dreams and when awake; the images had marked his entire life. And now came this pain, the pain of memories, caught by the camera and shown here in the heart of New York City, in the spectral room with its monitor that remembered everything. He clicked a key to close the images; the screen started flickering again, and the images were gone.

He looked around, and for the first time noticed another door, above which was written: *The Forgetting Room*. He hesitated for a moment and then decided to go in. He had barely touched the door before it swung wide open. He found himself in another room.

Hanging on the wall was a big board with instructions written in English. Albert read the text, translating it for himself into

Serbian. There are countless ways to achieve the act of forgetting. Arranged on the shelves running the length of the wall were different pills with their Latin names, fresh and pressed plants that ensure oblivion if properly used, different-coloured lights that help erase all trace of memory from the brain. It is a simple procedure, and the result is that you are guaranteed to forget completely.

For a moment Albert thought how much easier it would be if he could expunge this deep-rooted, persistent pain that he would not even have were it not for the memory of all the dark, disturbing, monstrous things that had comprised the better part of his life. But what would he do without that deep, penetrating pain? It held the memory of his father, his mother, Elijah. That pain was everything he was, and without it he, Albert Weisz, did not exist. Nor did the people he cared about most.

He felt drained; he could barely stand up, but he summoned the strength to go out into the fresh New York air. For a while he teetered like a drunk, holding on to the walls for support. Suddenly, off in the distance, he spotted the lights of his hotel and made for them. Ten minutes later he was walking through the door of the Marriott Hotel. The man at the reception desk barely glanced at him.

He was tired; he yearned for sleep – but not the kind that brought oblivion.

TWELVE

A child of violence

Uriel Cohen had tried to record the story of his life more than once. For years he had wanted to say what he knew about his family and its suffering, about the many, he believed, unknown details that could further illuminate the story of the Shoah. Numerous times he had sat down at his desk to write. In front of him were his mother's notes. In the tiny handwriting of an old lady she had described it all, so that nothing would be forgotten, writing just a few months before her death from angina pectoris. She died in her sleep, at night; she simply did not wake up one morning. It was Uriel who discovered her already cold, lifeless body.

Whatever he wrote seemed so banal; it had all been told so many times before. What he saw as his life could just be a big lie or perhaps a tangle of conflicting feelings – something that caused constant apprehension, unconnected to anything specific, an unease deeply entrenched in everyday life. Ever since he was a little boy he had been haunted by the idea that he would suddenly lose the power of speech and start forgetting words, that words would lose their meaning and become senseless sounds. The idea haunted him even more so now. There were so many things that could not be expressed in words; in most cases words were actually meaningless, they had become mendacious. A new language should be invented, one that was pure, unsullied, that would have clarity, depth, strength, that would be capable of expressing real feelings. Such a precise, forceful language would be the best defence against evil. 'Evil is terribly powerful, fearfully powerful, but it is also self-destructive,' Father Ivan of Sarajevo wrote in his diary.

In fact, all his life Uriel Cohen had walked in the shadow of all-embracing, powerful evil. Isaac Luria, the great Kabbalist, talked about the holiness of sin, about exile and redemption, about terrible internal exile, about how conquering the purest form of evil renews the world, elevating and organizing it in a way so that every individual corrects and betters himself. The individual act has universal meaning.

What is Judaism? Indeed, who is a Jew? First, it is someone whom others perceive as Jewish. Uriel remembered only too well his first day in high school. He was sitting at his desk, and his teacher, a tall, thin, fifty-year-old woman named Olga, was leafing through the register to familiarize herself with the names of her pupils when suddenly she stopped, pointed to a name in the book and said, 'Boys and girls, we've also got a foreigner in our class.' And she read out his name. All heads turned to look at Uriel, and his eyes welled up with tears. Although the teacher quickly realized her mistake, that first class was etched on his mind, and, in a way, it left its mark on him. Until that day he had had no particular awareness of himself. After that day he really was somehow a foreigner, even though he had been born in the country, spoke the same language as everybody else, had learned everything everybody else had learned. But the teacher's lapse, which had not really been a lapse at all, made him feel deep down inside that indeed he was somehow a foreigner, a foreigner in his own country, a foreigner among his friends, that he was 'different'. His schoolmates had normal names, whereas his sounded foreign to his ears, in a way almost indecent; no wonder the other teachers did not remember it correctly. Some of them called him Jakov, others Avram, some David; mostly they used such biblical, slightly unusual names. To tell the truth, he was hurt at first; he did not talk about it to anybody, not even his mother. But then he began to accept his awkward particularity as something unavoidable, something neither good nor bad, something that was simply a part of him, like his face, his height, the timbre of his voice . . . He became defiant and gradually turned into an eccentric, which in his later years narrowed down his circle of friends to only a handful of other 'foreigners'. If there was one thing Uriel had learned in life it was that anything was possible. The most extraordinary things could happen. Life could take a completely different turn in a single night or day; terrible, unpredictable misfortunes could happen, disasters caused by human madness or by something beyond our control could occur. When the time came even this planet of ours would disappear in an unimaginable cosmic explosion. What significance, then, could the life of a marginal creature, someone who is a foreigner in his own life, have? All the same, Uriel expected some sort of satisfaction, some sort of apology for everything done to him. It was not revenge he was seeking; he just wanted some sort of satisfaction. Otherwise his life had no meaning – and not just his life but the lives of others, not just his own personal and family history, but history *per se*, where historians keep looking for some sort of logic, trying to make sense of it. Movement, yes, but towards what? Towards an ideal society or towards the apocalypse? Or towards nothingness? Even after all these years somebody had to take the blame, somebody had to take responsibility for what happened.

Eliza, Uriel's mother, was sixteen when the war broke out in 1941. Eugen and Rosa Cohen, Eliza's parents, his grandparents, were doctors. At the start of the occupation, all Jewish doctors were dismissed from their jobs. Jews could only receive medical attention from other Jews. A number of Jewish clinics were organized. Eugene and Rosa worked in one such hospital clinic as well as in the Ashkenazi synagogue. Conditions in the hospital were dire: there were not enough beds, and they were short of basic drugs and medical supplies. But, because they worked in the hospital, Eugene and Rosa, unlike other Jews, were spared the dangerous, hard labour of extracting decomposing bodies from the rubble with their bare hands. The newspapers published two photographs of these workers wearing armbands that said *Jude*. In one, the guards had made them hold up four headless corpses; the other picture showed a dog the Jews had pulled out of the rubble being given a Jewish burial. It was the humour of the new age and the new authorities. Soon every day brought front-page news of executions. New anti-Jewish decrees were issued almost daily. Jews were prohibited from going to the theatre, the movies or other places of entertainment. They were banned from trams. The military command decreed that Jews had to hand in their radio sets or else face the harshest punishment. People wearing yellow armbands were increasingly harassed on the street. The mass arrest of men over the age of fourteen started at the end of the summer. Several times the occupying forces, supported by the

Special Police, stormed into hospitals and carted off the elderly and the sick. Nobody knew where they were taken or why. Much later people learned about the first Jewish death camp – Topovska Šuma – where much of Belgrade's male Jewish population was exterminated. Like others, Eugene and Rosa heard some of these stories, but they were random and full of such ghastly details that they did not want to believe them.

At the start of December Prime Minister Nedić's police went from house to house with orders for all remaining Jews to report to the Special Police for Jews in George Washington Street. The summons said that they should bring only as much luggage and linen as they could carry. They were to lock their apartment doors upon leaving, attach the keys of the apartment and basement to a card bearing their name and exact address and hand them over when reporting to the police. They were to bring with them cutlery, a blanket and a day's worth of food. Failure to report would be severely punished, the summons said.

On a freezing-cold December day hundreds of women, the elderly and children started reporting to the Special Police for Jews from all corners of Belgrade. They waited in line in the courtyard for all the formalities to be completed. Once this was done and they were registered, they were loaded on to open trucks and taken to the Sajmište. The trucks crossed the narrow pontoon bridge over the Sava River that replaced the big suspension bridge that had been destroyed.

Four rows of barbed wire enclosed the Sajmište concentration camp, ensuring that the inmates were completely isolated. Letters secretly smuggled out testified to the terrible living conditions and the growing number of the elderly and young who were freezing, starving and dying. It was impossible to hide the truth about the camp, and the few Jews whose jobs kept them outside the camp lived in fear of each new day. Working conditions in the Jewish hospital became almost impossible. Patients were lying in the corridors, in the open space on the ground floor, even in the courtyard. That first year of the war recorded one of the coldest winters ever. The Sava River froze over. Every day the people of Belgrade saw the makeshift wooden coffins of dead camp inmates being transported across the frozen river into the city.

Eugene and Rosa decided that Eliza should stop going to school. There had been instances of the police bursting into classrooms, removing Jewish children and turning them over to the Germans. Living on the ground floor of their building in Kosmaj Street were the caretaker Sima Andjus and his sick, bedridden wife. The Cohens arranged for him to look after Eliza in their absence, bring her lunch, check in on her and protect her in the event of any danger. But they were also worried about what they would do when the hospital closed down. In the early autumn they had thought that the situation would eventually improve, but now there was no room left for optimism. They were not sure what the best course of action would be. Eugene confided in the caretaker. They agreed to fix up a room in the basement. They bought some basic furniture – a bed, table, chairs – and put up a shelf with a few books in one corner. The room even had a small window that opened on to a shaft – just enough to provide a bit of fresh air. The door to this part of the basement was well concealed: only somebody who knew where it was could find it. They used the family jewellery to pay the caretaker. They did everything they could to ensure that the secret room remained hidden, but still it was risky. Hiding a Jew was punishable by death. They felt that they could count on the agreement they had reached with Andjus the caretaker, that she would be safe. They had known him for years; he had always been especially nice to Eliza, whom he had known from the day she was born, and in the good old days before the war, and even now when they could, the Cohens gave him the medicines needed for his severely ill, bedridden wife. All the same, it was a winter of constant worry and trepidation.

They saw in the new year of 1942 with a humble celebration in their fourth-floor flat. Andjus brought a bottle of brandy, eggs and sausages from his native village. The alliance forged between Andjus and the Cohens, a true conspiracy of silence, now formed a bond between them. They all wondered anxiously what the New Year would bring.

Eliza got used to being alone. She studied from her school books and dreamed of a normal life, always hoping that one day her isolation would come to an end. The grim winter days were long but spring was around the corner and it would resolve many dilemmas.

One day, someone he knew at the Special Police for Jews told Andjus that Rosa and Eugene Cohen had met a tragic end.

After taking Eliza to her hiding place, Andjus went up to the Cohen's fourth floor flat and collected all the valuables he could find, including a box containing a ring, a pearl necklace and a pouch of gold coins. He knew that either the Gestapo or the police would soon come around to seal off the flat, and he reasoned that it was better for him to take these things himself than to leave them for the police to find. He felt that this was only right and proper because there was a high price to pay for taking care of the Cohens' daughter.

Thus began Eliza's long period of captivity. She completely depended on Andjus. He came early every morning and every evening, bringing her food and concocted messages from her parents. Eliza cried until she had no tears left. Andjus's first few visits to the hideout were brief. He felt awkward in the girl's presence; she expected him to bring news of her parents, and he could not keep telling her the same old story. But soon his visits to the basement became an important part of his day – at least they took him away, if only briefly, from his own troubles, from his bedridden wife whose constant moaning was becoming increasingly hard to bear. He noticed that, as time passed, Eliza looked forward to his visits more and more eagerly; he was the only human being she could talk to, who could tell her what was happening in the outside world. And he, in comforting her, was glad to have someone to listen to him, to whom he meant something. Slowly but surely, he tried to get closer to Eliza; he developed a passion, perhaps even a lust for her. He had trouble explaining it even to himself. At first he had been put off by her helplessness, but then he started finding it perversely attractive. He made the difference between life and death. What he had initially found frightening now relieved him of any responsibility, any scruples. He started to see Eliza as a thing, as an object entirely in his possession. He was charmed and attracted by her youth, but now for the first time he also saw her as a woman, an attractive woman so different from his own hag of a bedridden wife who didn't look even human any more. For a long time he did not want to admit to himself what he felt for Eliza – a sick, warped, crude yet tender love. The first time he touched her hand and wiped away her tears with his handkerchief, the touch of her delicate, warm skin made him tremble. And in her desperate need to be comforted, she clung to him. She never dreamed what her touch meant to this strong, coarse man; she just felt a deep, growing pain from the stark loneliness of her life and the uncertainty of not knowing where her parents were. One evening he pounced on her like an animal, forced her to the ground and raped her. After that he would come every evening, without a word push her to the floor and rip off her clothes. Her initial helplessness and shock turned into anger; too weak to fight him, she bit and clawed at him, leaving teeth marks and scratches on his arms, and he reacted by slapping and punching her. In the end, on the verge of a nervous breakdown and madness, she was forced to accept the shameful, humiliating role of victim. There was no one to help or protect her. Eliza's entire life was reduced to terrible physical and moral suffering, to the four walls of the basement, to living with darkness and violence.

Uriel was born at the end of 1942. She named him after her grandfather, the cantor in Belgrade's synagogue. She bit off the umbilical cord herself. At first she wanted to drown this little creature born out of violence, this child of hate not love, but then she held him in her arms and would not let Andjus anywhere near him. The violent caretaker was baffled; he tried to persuade her to get rid of the child. Eliza knew him well by now. He was a bully, but he was spineless. She ignored his threats. And then, as the days passed, he started to change. He tried to win her over. He noticed that the boy looked like him. But Eliza shut herself off. He had ceased to exist for her. Little Uriel was raised in an atmosphere of hatred, without daylight; he learned to crawl and walk in this underground prison, in this reduced, confined, completely unfree world. But was the world outside free? For her and little Uriel, to step outside would mean to be deported to a death camp. Eliza had thought about it often enough: death could release her from this terrible, humiliating life of enslavement. But the birth of her son had driven away these thoughts. Now she dreamed that this child, who would one day be a man, would grow up to exact a high price for all their suffering. And, as thoughts of revenge took root in her mind, it helped her to endure, to persevere.

Little Uriel did not see daylight until he was three. One might say that he both metaphorically and literally crawled out of his semi-darkness into the light of day. It was like the greatest of miracles: streets, tall buildings, people, the sky, clouds, the sun – things he had not known even existed. He tottered on his little rickety legs, hanging on to his mother's skirt. Eliza had taken advantage of a careless moment on the part of her guard: he had forgotten to lock the door of her prison. For the past ten days he had heard the boom of cannon, bursts of machine-gun fire and shooting. He was scared, confused. The world was turning upside down again. Andjus disappeared. Later, his wife's decomposing body was discovered in one of the beds in his flat.

Eliza returned to the apartment upstairs on the fourth floor. She returned with her bastard son whom she both loved and hated. The neighbours avoided the once well-mannered, pretty little girl who in just a few years had utterly changed, both physically and mentally. She had become brusque, unpleasant, and there was something off-putting about her. Her face had coarsened, there were dark circles under her dead eyes; she was a frenzied little girl and tired old woman all in one and the same body. It was the kind of terrifying madness that horrified and frightened normal people. What did they know about the hell she had lived through? Her condition worsened when she learned of her parents' tragic end and the terrible truth that all her close and distant relatives were dead. For a few months she could not talk, she just mumbled, waving her arms around, frightening even her own unwanted child. Until, finally, she completely withdrew into herself, into an increasingly obvious alienation from the world, one that was no longer a passing state of mind but an exhausting state of unconcealed continuous suffering. She never told Uriel who his real father was or what had happened to him. As he got older he sensed that her story harboured a dark secret.

One day, in May 1952, somebody knocked at their door. Uriel opened it. Standing in front of him was a man with a long scruffy beard and ragged clothing. At the sight of Uriel he choked up before he could say anything.

Eliza appeared. She stood there dumbstruck and then started yelling, 'Get out of here! How dare you come here?'

She pushed Uriel back into the apartment and slammed the door shut. Trembling, she put her arms around him and squeezed him tight. That was when Uriel sensed, although he had no proof, that the tramp had something to do with his father. He never asked, and his mother never said a word about that day.

And so Uriel spent his early childhood in an atmosphere of suppressed unhappiness, with a secret past and, it is safe to say, a mentally disturbed mother.

When did Uriel become Jewish and how? That was a question that he, or Uri as his few friends called him, asked himself only much, much later. His mother never mentioned Judaism, nor had her tragically departed parents raised her in the Jewish tradition. In all matters they were and had thought of themselves as Serbs rather than Jews. They had seen themselves as assimilated, as Serbs of 'the faith of Moses'. And even that had been more of a non-committal, fading mark of distinction than a defining or religious trait. The anti-Semitism that had occasionally appeared had not concerned them; it was the anti-Semites' problem not theirs. They had forgotten the Ladino and Yiddish spoken by earlier generations, and their memories of the past had become hazy, lost in the mists of time. Even the solidarity with Jews fleeing pogroms in various European countries had gone. Eugene and Rosa had never viewed Palestine as their homeland, it had never even occurred to them to support Zionist ideas. They saw themselves as 100 per cent Serb. They had been shocked when at the start of the occupation they were forced to work in the Jewish hospital; they thought it must be some sort of mistake. Their lost 'Jewishness' was like a noose around their neck. Despite everything, they became Jewish again because others saw them as Jewish. And, in the end, they paid for it with their lives.

Uriel was Jewish only to the extent that others saw him as such, not because Eliza had raised him that way; on the contrary, she had done exactly the opposite. She felt nothing but anger and hatred for her origins. Belonging to a proscribed people had been the cause of all her troubles and suffering; it had killed her parents and threatened her child, a child who was her punishment, her unbreakable connection with the terrible past but also her greatest love.

TINNITUS

Dr Edo Pilsel finished his examination.

'Albert, sir, your ears are fine. That sound you hear doesn't come from the outside. It is within you. So deep inside you that no doctor can reach it. One in every five people has tinnitus. It's not an illness, it's a condition. You simply have to get used to this sound of a moving train and clattering wheels. If it's any consolation, some people who come to me hear roaring waterfalls, rolling thunder, wailing sirens. A moving train? It's just something you have to learn to live with.'

'No, doctor, I can't do that. To me, it's the worst sound there is. A sound I cannot get used to.'

NEWS

INVESTIGATION INTO PAINTINGS
THAT USE THE ASHES OF CAMP VICTIMS

WARSAW, 7 December 2012 – The Prosecutor's Office in Poland, in co-operation with the Swedish police, has launched an investigation into Swedish artist Carl Michael von Hausswolff following an exhibition of his work using the ashes of victims from the Majdanek German concentration camp, which, during the Second World War, was located in the eastern part of then occupied Poland.

An exhibition of watercolours by the controversial painter and composer opened in a private gallery in Lund, Sweden, at the beginning of December. Von Hausswolff mixed the watercolours with the ashes of Jews exterminated by the Nazis in Majdanek.

'I took some ashes from the oven in the crematorium during a visit in 1989. I didn't use it for any exhibition back then. It was too charged with the cruelty of its times. Two years ago I picked up the box of ashes and decided to do something with it. Figures started taking shape as if the ashes carried the energy, memories and souls of the tortured, the abused and the exterminated,' said the Swedish artist, speaking of the watercolours.

The exhibition led to protests in both Sweden and Poland, where the museum of the former Majdanek concentration camp compared this desecration of the victims' remains with stealing the *Arbeit Macht Frei* sign from the front gate of Auschwitz, the Nazis' biggest death camp, situated in the south of Poland.

THIRTEEN

*On his ninetieth birthday Emil Neifeld discovers that
remembering is more terrible than forgetting*

There are many things in my life that I would like to forget. But I can't. It's impossible. A Kabbalist once wrote: 'We are God's memory.'

Remembering is more terrible than forgetting.

I have never told anybody this before.

In Auschwitz I was a member of the *Himmel kommandos*, the 'black ravens', or the *Sonderkommandos* as we were known. After the victims were gassed, we of the *Himmel kommandos* went in and, once their gold teeth had been extracted, loaded the corpses on to carts and transported them to the ovens for incineration. Then we carried their ashes out in sacks and dumped them on the tip.

After a while I stopped feeling pity; all I felt was shame and guilt.

This is the first time I have ever talked about it. It was many years ago, but it is impossible to forget those horrific scenes. It is impossible to suppress something that has forever become a part of me.

I still wonder today: how did it all happen? We never thought such evil was possible. But, when it happened, we started getting used to it; it paralysed us, leaving us only with the strength to survive. Everything we once thought mad, unacceptable, impossible, became both possible and acceptable, because it had become our only reality. And there was no escaping it, for every other reality had been eradicated.

The evil we saw acquired a face, the face of the Gestapo. Evil exists only when it has a face. When it has physicality, the absolute power to crush, to destroy. Torture imprints itself on the victim's soul; nothing exists beyond the torture. It is the only reality there is. And the knowledge that evil exists causes pain, moral, psychological and physical pain.

Those of us who lived through it, the few of us who survived, never lost that feeling of humiliation and fear. Life wasn't life any more; it had lost all meaning. When you lose faith, when you lose hope, everything becomes muddled, and the result is a derangement verging on madness or depression. People did not commit suicide in the camps, they committed suicide after the camps, when they realized that they could not break free of the past. Once evil takes root it spreads and engulfs everything and everyone, the just and the unjust, the victim and the executioner. It changes and deforms everything.

The disintegration of one's inner soul translates into the loss of all meaning.

Only someone who has never experienced evil, never seen its true face, can deny its existence. 'The camp is a monstrous machine for reducing human beings to beasts,' wrote inmate Primo Levi.

What do we need after everything we have been through? Something very important, that we keep looking for in vain. What we need is a meaning for our suffering. But evil divests whatever it touches of meaning.

FOURTEEN

A letter about self-hate

Dear Uriel

I am only too familiar with the feeling that is troubling and upsetting you, the feeling of self-hate.

To be perfectly honest, self-hate is a typically Jewish syndrome. It manifests itself when social outsiders try to shed the heavy burden of 'otherness', of being 'different', when they try to break free from the often intolerable situation of being stereotyped by the majority. It is difficult, almost impossible, to do because the privileged majority does not accept changes to established stereotypes. There is no point in changing one's name or behaviour, in renouncing one's national or cultural ties or social position – an outsider always remains an outsider. Someone on the margins of society who, despite every effort and concession he makes, even renouncing his own basic identity, still fails to become an equal member of the community, expresses his discontent and despair through self-hate. He places most of the blame for his inability to become fully assimilated on himself and on his minority group. And so we arrive at the insane situation of having Jewish anti-Semites and Jewish Nazis. This same warped, pathological state of mind can be found among other minority and isolated groups and individuals, wherever there is no true equality or respect for differences.

For further reference, I recommend Broch's long essay on *Hofmannsthal and His Time*, Isaiah Berlin's essay on Moses Hess and Sander Gilman's monograph *Jewish Self-Hatred: Anti-Semitism and the Hidden Language of the Jews.*

Always at your service.

Best wishes

Emil Neifeld

P.S. Depending on the extent to which society has refused to accept us, we have all experienced this feeling of self-hatred. We want to be like everybody else, but they won't let us; our faith or the colour of our eyes marks us out as being different.

What else can we do but hate ourselves, hate that part of us that makes us different.

Dear Uriel

I feel I need to elaborate on my answer to your question.

Let me start by paraphrasing Professor Jan Assmann, who said that every forty years or so the past gets reinterpreted in the collective memory. The greatest evil of modern times is spoken of less fearfully today as other, 'greater' dangers are discovered. Witnesses die off, the lessons learned cease to inspire, the media – historians, too – follow the fashion or diktat of the politicians and, as Eric Hobsbawm wrote, rewrite history from the perspective of the present.

How many of us are left, sir, to bear witness to one of the most terrible periods in all of human history? Only a handful, and with each passing day our number is dwindling. My own end is near; shame will outlive me – like Kafka's protagonist: guilty yet guiltless.

You are of a different generation, the generation of our children, our sons and daughters, our grandchildren who know a little about it all from stories that cannot even remotely begin to describe the horror we lived through. It would take a non-existent language to tell the story properly. These are not my words, they are the words of Primo Levi and Jean Améry. They wrote them, and they committed suicide.

Solomon Levy also killed himself recently. He was uniquely, inimitably obsessed with exploring and revealing the true nature of evil, with doing what nobody had ever done before. He collected mounds of material, but, take my word for it, from Job's cries in the Bible to the present day, we have had no real answer to the question: what is evil, as a concept, as a notion, as life? There are times and places when you can almost touch it, when you can feel its icy breath, when it materializes. But no one, absolutely no one, has managed to truly define it. There is so much evil around us and in us, yet so few satisfactory descriptions as to what it actually is. Evil appears and is manifested in myriad ways, it takes countless forms, but no one has really described its *raison d'être*. Do you know what books that seek to resolve this question usually say? That evil is nothing specific, that it has no essence. And that instead of asking 'What is evil?' we should be asking 'Why is evil done?' I began to believe, and that belief has been corroborated, that there is a power, whether natural or unnatural, that is obstructing our access to important, truthful answers. People who have used their own experience to try to penetrate this prohibited sphere, have come to a more or less tragic end.

With the limited vocabulary of a child, one of the first questions I ever asked myself was why do people exist? The question obviously sounds absurd. But, my dear Uriel, I now realize that, even though the question was asked with the naïvety of a child, it remains unanswered to this day, despite the fact that it has been pondered by the greatest minds. Similarly, there is no answer to the question of why evil exists. Some people respond by lending evil a metaphysical dimension rooted in the obscure realm of the mysterious and the occult. However, my dear Uriel, our lives are shrouded in mystery. There are some things that we simply cannot understand; our minds are just not capable of it.

FIFTEEN

*In which Uriel Cohen discovers
the existence of a 'phantom observer'*

Dear Emil

I don't feel well. The older I get the more prone I am to troubling thoughts. When I was younger I managed to cope with them somehow. Perhaps I believed that time heals, as they say. I am becoming increasingly anxious; this constant unease has become an almost physical pain. I used to think of indifference as a sin, but now I would welcome it as a salvation. I have neither self-respect nor self-confidence; all I have is fear, fear of I don't know what or who, but it fills me body and soul, it fills my every day, from dawn to dusk, it even manifests itself in my dreams, and it will be like that until the very end, if ever there is an end, if there are no new trials and tribulations awaiting us over there in that unknown world. This endlessness, with no new beginnings and the constant repetition of misery, is a terrible thing to behold.

I read somewhere that people are preparing to launch a great war against the forces of darkness and that it will end in anarchy. A glacial winter will engulf the earth, and the shadow of huge apocalyptic beasts will block out the sun. The forces of evil will take over, fires will break out and eventually the whole world will sink to the bottom of the sea. They say that all living things will inevitably come to such an end; it is simply destined to be. And then, say these prophesies, a new world will rise up from the sea, a world where goodness, not evil, shall prevail, where there will be no room for us, for as we emerged in evil so we shall disappear with evil.

Even if such a thing should happen – at present these are merely predictions based on various national myths – is that any consolation? Consolation that everything will go back to the nothingness it came from, that everything will be voided as if it never happened. If that occurs, then why this senseless, unwarranted suffering that rules our lives?

I don't know, my dear Emil, what to call the reality I am living. It is a disease, a disease that must have a medical name. I don't know if you have ever felt what I feel, that my every move, even my most secret thought is monitored, followed, that this 'phantom observer' definitely exists. Quietly, calmly, my double watches me sink ever deeper into my own darkness, finding a kind of perverse, lurid pleasure in doing so. Perhaps I am wrong to call him my double. I don't know where he comes from or who has sent him, but he is always here to denigrate every genuine feeling I have, to mock and ridicule the depth and extent of my illness. How can one live with something like that? With a face in the mirror that is everything I am not but from which there is no escape? Can I possibly be that other face as well, that shadow, that ghost that is driving me mad, that is taking me to dark places, that keeps reminding me that I am an unwanted child, a 'bastard' as my mother used to call me in her moments of madness and despair?

I am sure you would help me if there were a way. That we would help one another if we could. But we each bear our own pain and are captive to our own doubts; we each carry our own cross and die alone.

Sometimes, but only sometimes, words become bridges that bring us together.

Please do not take this the wrong way, but I see you as the father I never had, the father I always wanted to have.

Yours

Uriel Cohen

NEWS

GERMAN NEUROLOGIST CLAIMS TO HAVE DISCOVERED THE AREA OF THE BRAIN WHERE 'EVIL' LURKS

Bremen scientist Dr Gerhard Roth says the 'evil patch' lies in the brain's central lobe and shows up on X-rays as a dark mass.

The dark mass at the front of the brain appears in all scans of people with records of criminal violence. When you look at the brain scans of hardened criminals there are almost always severe shortcomings in this part of the brain. There is no doubt that this is the area of the brain where evil forms and lurks.

Roth divides criminals into three groups: the first is made up of 'psychologically healthy' people who grow up in an environment where it is 'OK to abuse, steal and murder'; the second is the mentally disturbed criminal who sees his world as threatening; and the third group consists of 'pure psychopaths'.

SIXTEEN

An unexpected visit; Albert Weisz learns of
Solomon Levy's secret

It was that time of day when the light recedes into twilight before the darkness of night sets in. A time when things lose their daytime contours, acquire shadows and change shape. The perfect time for apparitions and ephemeral nocturnal creatures.

Somebody was ringing Albert's doorbell. He felt a chill down his spine. Who could it be? For a second he thought of not answering, of disappearing, of not being there for the uninvited guest. Albert had no contact with his neighbours, he had nothing to do with the authorities and he had no relatives who could surprise him with a visit. But the stranger kept ringing that doorbell. Then he knocked on the door, and there was a scratching noise, like a cat clawing.

When Albert tentatively opened the door he found himself face to face with a tall, thin, deathly pale stranger with dark, sunken eyes. Judging from the liver spots on his face, he must have been quite old. As soon as the man spoke, Albert recognized the voice that kept waking him up in the dead of night.

'Albert, sir, may I come in?'

In lieu of an answer, Albert stepped aside and waved the stranger in. Friend? Foe? In the end it didn't matter; there were worse things than this that he couldn't deal with, so he might as well let the spectre into his apartment and into his life. Was he a real person or just a figment of his imagination?

'My name won't mean anything to you, so I will not introduce myself.' The stranger's voice faded in and out, sometimes dropping to a whisper, as if his whole organism was slowly giving up. 'I've come to fulfil a duty, to carry out Solomon Levy's request.'

He took from his bag a box decorated with mysterious signs, obviously the symbols of a sect. Albert remembered that somebody had sprayed one of those symbols on the front door of Solomon Levy's building and that he had later seen it again, this time made from pebbles, on his friend's grave.

'Solomon asked me to give you this upon his death.'

Albert quietly took the box. He looked at the symbols, perplexed.

'Solomon Levy was a Dönmeh.'

'A Dönmeh? What's that?'

'We Dönmehs are followers of Sabbatai Zevi. We number several thousand and secretly follow his teachings.' The stranger paused for a moment.

'We accept Judaism and Islam. We are not converts, although there are those who call us that. We take our teachings from the Kabbalah.'

'You knew Solomon, you say?'

The stranger nodded. 'I knew him well,' he replied with the faintest of smiles. He turned away, as if he had already said too much. Without glancing at Albert he headed for the door, wanting to disappear from Albert's life as quickly as possible now that he had completed his task. 'Goodbye, sir.'

Albert opened his mouth to ask him something, but it was too late.

The stranger quickened his step and disappeared almost noiselessly down the stairs. Albert had Solomon Levy's box in his hands. He examined it carefully from every side. Hesitating only briefly, he opened the box.

Inside was a letter.

SEVENTEEN

*The confession of Solomon Rubenovich; the box
with the letter is opened on Yom Kippur*

Albert, my friend, forgive me. We live with deceptions. And I am just one deception more. Solomon Levy is not my real name. My real name is Solomon Rubenovich. My father was Ruben Rubenovich. If the mention of his name makes you tremble, please, I beg you, read this letter through to the end.

I grew up in a family of pious Jews. I was raised to obey the laws of the Halakha, to go to temple on holidays and light a candle on Shabbat. No, we were not orthodox Jews, none of us was, but our religion and our traditions were important to us.

I was a frail, sickly child, and my parents always worried about me. Most of their prayers were for my health. And, truly, when I see myself in the few surviving photographs of those days, I look almost translucent, not like a boy but like the ghost of a boy who could be blown away by the slightest breeze.

But I can say without false modesty that what my body lacked my mind made up for in spades. By the age of ten I already spoke several languages: Yiddish, Hebrew, French and English. I learned languages so quickly and easily that people thought I was marked for greatness. We had a rich library of books; it was the only wealth we had, our family legacy, and so from early childhood I was able to satisfy my thirst for reading, at first with whatever came to hand because for me every book was a world of wonders. I read even when I comprehended little of what I was reading; I understood it in my own way. Reading gave me an inner joy as I was growing up, when my precarious health kept me mostly at home because my parents were afraid that all sorts of deadly diseases were lurking outside. I talked to the books, confided in them, lived with them; books filled the huge void of having no friends my own age. In a way, I was closed off from life, and yet full of the life described in books, which I began to believe was the only real life there was.

Anyway, they say we are a people of books, and I had literally come to depend on them. Some of these books, those that I loved especially, were very old. Sometimes, turning the yellowed pages, I thought they might at any moment disintegrate into dust, that is how old they were. I remember some of their titles: the 1671 *Biography of Sabbatai Zevi* by Solomon Leib Katz and the *History of Sabbatai Zevi* by Nahum Bril, published in Vilnius in 1879.

My first taste of real excitement came when I read about the life and work of the mystic Sabbatai Zevi and his follower and advisor Nathan of Gaza. I was greatly taken by the story of the great mystic who mobilized the entire Jewish world and travelled to numerous European countries and cities announcing the imminent coming of the Messiah.

Shut up in my little room and with an active imagination, I saw myself making similar journeys and dreamed of an adventurous life with a mission that would reveal to me the power of belief and the purpose of existence.

When I was very small I asked my parents a simple question that they were unable to answer and probably thought was childish and naïve: why do we exist; why are we here? The question kept gnawing at me and demanded an answer. Many years later Sabbatai Zevi's life and fate provided me with a kind of answer that might not have satisfied everyone, but it did me. I discovered the cosmic meaning of my own existence. I needed to help vanquish the evil that had emerged with the creation of the world and contribute to establishing a just world where the Jews would no longer be in perpetual exile, in *galut*.

Zevi based his teachings and movement on Isaac Luria's Kabbalah and 'the breaking of the vessels', the mystic explanation for the persecution of the Jews and their deliverance from the damnation of exile.

When the world was being created, divine light streamed into the void of nothingness and filled it with creative light. However, the vessels receiving that light were not strong enough to contain it, and they broke, they shattered into thousands of pieces, and evil pervaded the world. Their shards fell into the deep demonic abyss. Worlds collapsed in the ensuing chaos. Everything that happens is a consequence of the breaking of the vessels. Evil shall be vanquished, the world shall be restored to its originally envisioned state and the Jews and their God shall cease being persecuted when the vessels are repaired. Through his actions, every Jew takes part in repairing these vessels. Repairing the world brings salvation.

In short, we live in an unfinished world dominated by evil in anticipation of a world of hope, goodness and love. This simplified picture of the creation and repair of the world has become my own guiding belief. As the life of Sabbatai Zevi shows, this has been a journey of trials and tribulations, and of what is called 'the holiness of sin'.

Here I want to say a few words about my father. Ever since I was little, he stood for me as an example of a respected, righteous, pious Jew. I saw him as the incarnation of Sabbatai Zevi. When I came of age my father told me that he belonged to a secret group of the Jewish Messiah's followers and that he was taking the great mystic's path of trial and tribulation. But let me return to the teaching of 'the holiness of sin'.

In 1666, when Sabbatai, recognized as the Messiah by the Jewish people, arrived in Constantinople to remove the crown from the sultan's head and proclaim the dawn of a new messianic age and a new kingdom on earth, he was arrested by the Turkish authorities. But they did not kill him as expected. He was taken to a prison near Gallipoli. Several months later, in the presence of the sultan, Sabbatai Zevi abandoned Judaism and converted to Islam. Nathan of Gaza, his loyal disciple, explained the magnitude of this act: in order to take part in repairing the world it is not enough to perform only good deeds; one must descend to the darkest depths of the most terrible evil and confront it, one must experience the terrible fate of the exile. That is what the Messiah did. He descended into hell itself so that he might touch it with his holiness. He seemed to become a Moslem, but in fact he was more Jewish than ever. And, ever after, he lived his life in two worlds. One was the world yet to come, and the other the world that is. One must touch evil in order to change and vanquish it.

I mention the life of Sabbatai Zevi to make it easier to understand my own life story. No small number of people accepted his teachings, and after he died they followed his path, either publicly or secretly.

I, indeed, am one of them.

I had to mention this in order for you to understand what follows. Everything my father did in his life was done out of deep, true conviction, never out of cowardice or weakness.

And it was the same on that summer's day in 1942 when he was arrested and taken to the Serbian Special Police and to its chief, Dragi Jovanović, personally. Following the executions in Topovska Šupa and exterminations at the Sajmište camp, Serbia was already *judenfrei*, cleansed of Jews. There were just a small number that the Gestapo and Serbian Special Police had failed to trace. They used false documents and hid, concealed and protected by loyal friends. But they lived in constant fear of discovery because hiding Jews was punishable by death and not many people were prepared to risk it.

(I stopped writing at this point. It was past midnight, and suddenly I felt tired. I tossed and turned in bed, drenched in sweat. I had to take a sedative. However, I was visited not by the sandman but by fragments of the story that I wanted to tell. But how could I write about it truthfully and persuasively? How could I describe it calmly, rationally, credibly? So now here I am, rising before dawn after a sleepless night, continuing this testament of a letter to you, my dear friend.)

To this day I don't know who turned us in. We thought they had forgotten about us and that with our forged documents we were safe in our hiding place on the outskirts of town.

As I said, my father was brought to the Chief of the Serbian Special Police. They did not torture him, they were civil, inasmuch as that was possible at a time when Jews were proscribed. My father knew some of the police officers, his erstwhile fellow-citizens, now the arbiters of life and death.

'Help us, and we will spare your family.'

They put him in solitary confinement and gave him all of the next day to think it over. More than enough time. No, it was not the promise that my mother and I would be spared that decided it for him. Of that I am certain. I knew my father. He saw the offer as a message from a much higher authority than the Special Police. He took his decision not because he wanted to save his neck or ours, although he loved us as only the best of husbands and fathers could. He took it to save everybody. To save humanity, I'd say. As Nathan of Gaza put it, you have to hit rock bottom, the very depths of hell, in order to emerge pure and unblemished, as God's sinner, marked by the holiness of sin. You cannot know goodness until you know evil.

The biggest sacrifice my father willingly made towards this end was to renounce, not for ever, just for that moment, all that a decent man holds dear: his honour, his pride and his reputation. He renounced his vanity. His only fear, he later told me, was the magnitude of the sacrifice he would have to make.

He accepted the offer.

He knew all the leading members of our small community in town. On holidays he attended service in the synagogue. Prominent Jews from our town and from all over the country often called on him for advice, following the old tradition of seeking the advice of those who were older, wiser, respected. Such had been the custom in his native Lemberg, where his father, my grandfather, the honourable tzadik, had held court. I often listened to these conversations with my father from the wings, pleased with his wise answers.

We left our hiding place and returned to our apartment in what was now a deserted building. Our neighbours had vanished without a trace. The library had been looted. There were no books about Sabbatai Zevi any more, but his spirit lived on in our house.

Early in the morning a limousine came to pick my father up. He put on his best suit. Agents were waiting for him in front of the house. They accompanied him to 'work'. They stopped at the train and the bus stations and waited for the arriving and departing passengers. My father's sole task was to identify Jews with false papers, to point them out, the rest of the job was up to the police and the Gestapo. I don't know how many times he did it, very few of our people were left, but the trade in forged documents enabled even that small number to slip through the various checkpoints

No matter. He became what was called a 'collaborator of the occupiers', an informer; he had sold his soul. I know none of it was true, he was just a 'holy sinner', a follower of the teachings of Sabbatai Zevi, profoundly convinced that the sacrifice he made by touching the very depths of evil was simply a way to surmount it. There were tears in his eyes when he returned home late at night. He sacrificed himself, but he also left a mark on us, on my mother and me.

A few times I stole out of the house and secretly tailed my father going to 'work'. He would stand at the entrance to the train station, both saint and sinner, paying the highest of prices for his awful deed. How could anybody understand it when even I, his own son, felt that he was doing himself and others a terrible wrong. To understand is to justify. I did understand him up to a point, because Sabbatai Zevi lived inside me as he did inside him, but I also felt ashamed, so much so that I could not look him in the eye when he came home at night.

That is my story, dear friend, a story I am now revealing to you. It is the true story of my family and me. I owe it to you because of our long years of friendship, when we confided our most private thoughts to one other. But some things we never said, because no one can ever say everything. My mother could not bear the magnitude of my father's monstrous sacrifice. She had a nervous breakdown and died in a mental asylum. My father had collaborated in the terrible conviction that this was part of the price to be paid for general redemption. Unlike the people he had collaborated with, he refused to flee. He committed suicide just before the end of the war.

But before that, he obtained forged papers and a new name for me so that I could start life as somebody who had been miraculously saved from extermination, so that I could resume life with a false biography.

Forgive me for having deceived you. It took me a long time to realize that even after all these years, little has changed since the Shoah. Hardly anything, really; people are still killing each other, and the innocent are still dying. I have decided to disappear, to set all my illusions on fire, including myself.

I leave only this letter. Have pity on my soul and on my sins. The 'holiness of sin' does not exist nor does descending into the very depths of primordial evil help to repair the world. Evil is a hundred times stronger and more powerful than goodness. We are condemned to eternal *galut*, to eternal exile.

On this day of Yom Kippur, the day of prayer for acknowledging, confessing and forgiving sins, please, dear friend, say a prayer for the salvation of my soul.

EIGHTEEN

It all seems like a hallucination

Misha Wolf listened to Albert's story.

'So, your visitor was the mysterious man who had been following you?'

'I think so. I recognized the voice.'

'And you let him in and then let him leave just like that?'

'I did.'

The professor smiled. 'And he was no monster? Somebody from the other world? From another planet?'

'I don't know who or what he was. He didn't talk about himself. And I didn't ask.'

'C'mon, admit it, you saw in him the Devil himself. You must have been disappointed.'

'Maybe it really was Satan, or one of his creatures.'

'Come on, Albert. Drop these fantasies of yours.'

Albert fell silent. He was in two minds as to whether to tell the music professor the whole truth. Not a word about Solomon Levy, that's to say Solomon Rubenovich, about the heirs of Sabbatai Zevi, about the holiness and monstrosity of evil. That story he kept to himself, a story few could fully understand, because he did not fully understand it himself.

Misha Wolf rose to his feet and walked over to the bookcase that covered the whole wall from top to bottom. He scanned the books, looking for something. He pulled an old tattered book with loose pages off the shelf.

'This is where I wrote down some of my own experiences. And those of others.' He found a page. '"Some thoughts we are not conscious of can turn into ghosts." So wrote De Quincy.' He fell silent for a moment. 'That is why, dear friend, we do not have the right to say "This isn't true; things like that don't happen." All these things happen in our minds. Both good and bad. All these apparitions, vampires, werewolves, the physical form that evil can take, they are all in our minds.'

If he expected Albert to agree, he was disappointed. Albert had the impression that even the music professor did not entirely believe his own words, that his refusal to confront the powers of evil was down to cowardice and the fear of what he might discover.

'Your own case, the case of our friend Solomon Levy, all these cases of a dwindling generation where soon no living witness will be left to attest to the terrible evil we lived through, they are all material for a psychiatrist. Both the people who committed evil against us and we who experienced that evil. There is no evil without people, remember that and forget all these stories about the metaphysics of evil. As far as I am concerned, evil is a kind of madness, a disease, an aberration, an obsessive need to destroy. You will agree that nature is not perfect. I say this, dear Albert, to free you from your phantasms which, because of your personal traumas, you are turning into mythical monsters. Illness is dangerous, and madness is dangerous, but both can be controlled.'

Albert looked down; he did not know what to say.

Misha Wolf told him firmly, 'Get some rest. Get out of town for a while. A change of scenery will do you good.' He continued, his tone softer now, almost beseeching, 'Take my advice.'

Albert hesitated for a moment, then he nodded and squeezed his friend's hand.

'Of course. You're probably right. Maybe that's the way to get rid of my nightmares.'

Albert Weisz writes in his notebook:

This is all starting to look like a hallucination; maybe it really is a hallucination, an illusion, there's no proper name for it. This unbearable feeling of guilt because of my brother Elijah. Guilt for not having found him, for having abandoned him on that freezing cold night. From the day I was born my whole life has been one continuous despairing nightmare.

Whatever the case, I accepted the advice to leave, to travel, to get rid of my paranoia, to remove myself, if only temporarily, from this environment that was pressuring me until I felt I would explode, to escape these relentless apparitions, if apparitions they were.

I looked through the tourist brochures. One caught my eye:

Travel Resumes on the Orient Express!

On 4 October 1883 a steam train departed from the railway station in Strasbourg, taking its carriages to faraway Romania. That train was called the Orient Express, and it took forty passengers along as special guests.

The company soon gained a reputation for offering its passengers adventure combined with luxury.

Aristocrats, prominent figures and the famous travelled on the Orient Express to Vienna, Budapest, Bucharest and cities across the very heart of Europe.

The many secrets and mysteries surrounding the famous train have become the stuff of legend.

We are reviving the glory of the Orient Express. The most luxurious travel for the most discerning customers!

EPILOGUE

Through the darkness of night
Through landscapes bathed in moonlight
Past slumbering stations
The train rushes on

Albert Weisz is on the train.

His ticket is still in his right hand. He folds it in half and carefully puts it into his pocket. His seat number is printed on the ticket. This is important because bureaucrats have been known to issue two tickets for the same seat.

The carriage looks perfectly decent and its passengers civil. All the seats are occupied. Twelve seats and twelve passengers.

He tries to remember whether the number has some symbolic or mystical significance. It is the number of God's people. Jacob's twelve sons are the ancestors of the eponymous twelve tribes of Israel. Celestial Jerusalem has twelve gates. The number twelve separates the world of the good from the world of the bad. On the other hand, Albert thinks how stupid it is to look for a symbolic meaning in everything. Things are simply what they are, to quote professor Misha Wolf; they usually have no deeper meaning.

This time his thoughts are interrupted by the high-pitched voice of the man sitting next to him. He is pointing at the brass plate above the seats, which says:

The remaining car was constructed by the
Pullman Car Company at its
Longhedge Works in South London.
The livery applied by the Pullman Car Company
was as applied to the
South Eastern & Chatham Railways.

The celebrated company guarantees a safe and comfortable journey because, as the passenger happily explains, carriages like this are not made any more, except for adventure-filled journeys such as this one. Everything is done to ensure a comfortable and safe trip for the passengers, a trip that will remind them of the good old days, of an age when comfort was of prime importance. The seats turn into beds with ease, and in the corner of the carriage there is a small kitchen where you can make things like tea, so convenient for mothers with small children. In fact, there is a couple with two children in their compartment. The five-year-old boy has his face pressed against the window, and the little girl, who is no more than two, is clutching her mother, frightened by the repetitive clatter of the wheels and the occasional whistle of the locomotive sounding its warning call, as prescribed by the rules of the railway. The man closes his eyes, hoping to sleep, but the woman stares over the boy's head out into the night as if with a sense of foreboding. All mothers, thinks Albert, are preoccupied with their apprehensions and fears: they want to protect and feed their children and see them grow into free, proud human beings; they want to overcome illness and misfortune, because people have everything working against them. That's what Albert thinks.

Through the darkness of night
Through landscapes bathed in moonlight
Past slumbering stations
The train rushes on.

It is only now that Albert notices the passenger wrapping his shoulders with a tasselled tallit prayer shawl, white with blue and black stripes at either end. The man places a kippah on his head and recites a prayer whose words are hard to understand. His murmuring and the monotonous turning of the train's wheels are the only sounds to be heard.

He finishes his ritual and returns the kippah and shawl to his valise. He catches the look of curiosity on the face of the man with the high-pitched voice.

'Are you religious?' asks the elderly Jewish man.

The other man shakes his head, 'No, I am an atheist.'

The old man smiles. 'An atheist, you say. So, you don't believe in anything.'

'I only believe in what I can understand.'

'Well, that explains why you don't believe in anything!'

For a moment they both fall silent. Then the atheist says, 'After everything that's happened, what is there left to believe in? God cannot exist if he allowed his chosen people to perish.'

'So, you are a Jew who doesn't believe.'

'That's right, sir. Do you know the story of the rebbe of Sadigura? Every Saturday the Almighty reportedly descended from heaven to recite the holy prayers with the rebbe. A man who doubted the story asked the person who was spreading it just how he knew it was true. "There's not a doubt in the world," replied the latter. "The rebbe himself confirmed it." "But how do you know that the rebbe was telling the truth?" "Do you think the Almighty would have anything to do with a liar?" came the answer.'

The elegant man sitting in the corner of the compartment wipes his damp brow with a handkerchief. Until then he had seemed to be dozing, uninterested in his fellow passengers.

'Haven't you noticed, gentlemen,' he says suddenly, 'that there is something frightening about travelling at night?'

For all his elegance, his wan face and narrow frame give the impression of ill health.

'Here, look out the window. The night is all around; it covers everything – fields, hills, everything is shrouded in complete darkness,' he laughs. His laughter sounds more like wheezing than amusement.

And the night is indeed all around, including in the souls of these people whom fate has brought together on this romantic journey into the heart of Central Europe, people who are increasingly filled not with the excitement of travel but with inexplicable trepidation. It is not clear what they are afraid of or why. Instead of talking about the beauty of Central Europe's venerable cities, of sights that with the rising morning sun will dazzle their eyes, they are speaking about their own misfortunes and those of others, and they are doing so less and less casually, if ever casual they were.

And were it already daybreak so that they could see the landscape rolling past them, their trepidation might be justified. Racing along newly laid tracks, the Orient Express passes by destroyed and torched stationmaster's houses. You do not have to be an expert in logic or a politician or understand relations between nations and states to ask, why destroy something that will one day have to be rebuilt? It is a question any rational person would ask, not just passengers taking a nostalgic trip on the legendary train.

Since it has become a night of confidences, it is now the turn of the jittery passenger who keeps getting up, opening the door of the compartment and looking out into the empty corridor. As the others are about to hear, he suffers from obsessive-compulsive disorder; he thinks he alone is to blame for the disaster in India when landslides destroyed entire villages, killing many people. He says that it would never have happened if, when he left the house that day, he had not bypassed the pedestrian crossing he otherwise always used. Everything is interconnected, and any out-of-the-ordinary move we make causes unexpected, often cataclysmic disturbances. Prior to the disaster, he says, he was a perfectly normal person. Now he carries this huge feeling of guilt for the death of so many people. As the Orient Express races through the night, something suddenly happens to these people whom fate has thrown together. Fear starts to creep into their souls.

Experiments with mice have shown, and subsequent tests on human beings have confirmed, that the sensory organs can detect fear. But even scientists have been unable to discover where fear actually comes from. The senses merely signal that a situation can quickly become threatening and dangerous.

The conductor appears at the door of the compartment. He has the same uniform that conductors used to wear in times past. And he has the standard Orient Express bag slung over his shoulder.

He greets them politely and asks for their tickets. All the passengers, including Albert, have their tickets ready. Only the couple with two children nervously rummage for them in their bags.

The conductor says kindly, 'Please, take your time. We're in no hurry.'

Eventually they find their tickets. The conductor perforates them with his little machine. At first he doesn't seem interested in the passengers' conversation. But when the man with the high-pitched voice starts saying that the world is based on human solidarity and on the conscience of individuals, he starts paying attention. At one point the conductor takes the unexpected and unusual step of joining in.

'You are completely mistaken, sir. Yours are the words of a delusional pacifist who believes in the just order of things. The people who change our world are not those who want order, justice and peace. They are those who are said to have no conscience. Those who have no mercy or morals. Only the weak call for a conscience and fairness. That, if you will allow me, is my profound belief. Luckily for humanity, people without a conscience, ready to do anything, account for nearly 10 per cent of the population.'

The man with the high-pitched voice becomes agitated. His voice rises even higher. 'No, *you* are mistaken. People without a conscience are secret psychopaths, well adapted to their environment until certain circumstances make them reveal their true violent, cold-hearted nature, a nature devoid of empathy and marked by unrestrained aggression . . . People without a conscience are, by the very nature of things, pathological criminals.'

The conductor laughs disdainfully. 'You, sir, are one of those people who would like to preserve the existing order for ever. It makes you feel safe, and so you would keep it for the next hundred, maybe even thousand years . . .' he sneers. 'But changing the world also means, of course, committing crimes, torching villages and towns, killing civilians . . . That's the price of change and without change there can be no progress . . .'

'Progress? What progress? Progress in doing evil, in committing crimes . . . ?'

The man with the high-pitched voice is about to say something, but the conductor simply waves him away, not wanting to get into an argument. 'We are approaching the tunnel. Close the windows, please!'

> Through the darkness of night
> Through landscapes bathed in moonlight
> Past slumbering stations
> The train rushes on.

The long whistle of the locomotive. The train enters the tunnel. The lights in the carriage go out. The system has crashed some-where. But the passengers have no one to complain to. They have been left on their own, and slowly they begin to panic.

The tunnel seems to take for ever. No one says a word. But the animal fear grows, fear of the total darkness with no stars or moonlight, fear of the mountain's womb they are travelling through.

The little boy cries out, 'Mummy, why is there no light?'

The weak flame of a match momentarily illuminates the passen-gers' anxious faces. Someone opens the window, letting in the pungent smell of smoke, causing everyone to cough. The weak light is short-lived. They are again plunged into pitch-black dark-ness.

Finally, the train emerges into the light of day and a snowy morning. The sudden whiteness seems eerie, unreal. The fields are blanketed with snow, and spectral mountains can be seen in the distance through the morning mist.

Albert rubs his eyes. The sudden whiteness gives him a headache. The train slows down as the locomotive snorts its way past the snow-drifts. As far as Albert can remember, the travel brochure made no mention of possible bad weather.

The man in the corner seat of the compartment, who keeps wiping his perspiring, pockmarked face with a handkerchief, takes a book out of his bag. In a voice of almost suppressed rapture he reads out an excerpt from Stefan Zweig's *The World of Yesterday*: "'There was no country to which one could flee, no quiet which one could purchase; always and everywhere the hand of fate seized us and dragged us back into its insatiable play.'"

Albert wants to protest. Why that particular excerpt? There are so many other things worth quoting.

The man with the pockmarked face bursts into almost maniacal laughter, 'No, it's no coincidence that we met here, in this place. We are losers. For us, this world is the world of Satan.'

The boy keeps crying. His mother tries to soothe him. Everybody is talking at the same time. Albert can't make out the words. All these nasal, high-pitched, sharp voices of adults and children are making such a racket. Not to mention the clattering of the train's wheels.

Da-da-Dum-da-da-Dum-da-da-Dum.

Albert cannot stand the noise; he's no longer sure if it is real or only in his head.

He steps out into the corridor, but the noise persists. He plugs his ears with his fingers, but it is just as loud, and getting louder.

He peers through the door of the other compartment. He recognizes some of the passengers: Uriel Cohen in a grey flannel suit, his eyes at half-mast; the balding Misha Wolf, his violin case on his knees; the crowd from New York, from the Marriott Hotel, the abandoned, forsaken children of Central Europe. What a strange, unexpected coincidence. Everybody on the same train, the same journey! All born under an unlucky star. That is the only thing that unites them.

Da-da-Dum-da-da-Dum-da-da-Dum.

He tries to open the compartment door and join them. The door is locked. He bangs on it with his fist, but it is no use. They do not hear him, their minds are elsewhere, turned inwards; they do not notice him.

He walks to the end of the corridor and opens the connecting door to the next carriage.

The rumble of the moving train mingles with the noise that has been hounding him; the cold winter air, the wind and the snow-flakes make him shiver, and he hurries to open the door of the next carriage. There he finds himself in semi-darkness, reeling from the stench of human bodies. He steps on a hand, hears somebody yowl and quickly steps back but trips over another body. There's no room for him to move. The floor is carpeted with people; he hears their moaning and muffled cries.

The tourist trip is turning into a nightmare, the Pullman carriage into a cattle truck.

Suddenly, the Orient Express slows down. Albert somehow manages to push his way to the wood-panelled wall of the carriage. A faint ray of light is showing through a slit between two planks of wood. He peers through it and sees a small provincial railway station crowded with people moving right and left like shadows. Poorly dressed for the cold weather and toting bundles. He hears loud, unintelligible, menacing shouts and dogs barking. Uniformed soldiers line the way. The train pulls to a stop with a long-drawn-out whistle. Its doors open, letting in a blast of freezing air.

He is at a provincial train station like the one he saw in his dream. There is the illegible name of the station beneath the dirty windows, and staring out at the platform are the station workers, their distorted faces looking more feral than human. The plaster is peeling off the walls of the stationmaster's house; everything is in a state of decay. Only now it is not a dream, it is the real thing. And the station is not deserted, it is crowded with people being escorted by armed men, moving along a well-trodden path towards the big, green, wide-open gate of the camp.

Above the gate the sign says: *ARBEIT MACHT FREI.*

THE HIDDEN ORDER

Albert shuts his eyes. That is how you become invisible. That is the incredible trick his father used to talk about. One worthy of their celebrated relative Houdini, the greatest escape artist of all time.

'This world of ours is not exactly the most perfect place to live in,' his father used to say. 'When you find yourself in trouble, just shut your eyes and wait.'

Look, it's true. He is not in that queue any more. He is in a snowy-white landscape calling out to Elijah. And, from far off, Elijah's young, sweet voice answers back. Out of the snowy sky comes a white horse with the head of a dog, and riding it, holding tightly on to its mane, is Elijah. The horse with the head of a dog alights noiselessly on to the snowy field. Elijah runs into his brother's arms.

It is the moment of joy and redemption that Albert has been dreaming of, a moment it has been worth living for, waiting for.

They walk off, hand in hand, Elijah looking lovingly at his older brother.

An endless snowy plain opens up before them.

The shadows of two human figures emerge from the morning mist. Their parents. They and the boys run towards each other.

They are together again. Isaac and Sara embrace Albert and Elijah. Nobody will ever separate them again. Nobody, not ever.

That is all he wanted. A world without pain, injustice or despair. A world without evil.

Such a world does exist – in a different, hidden order of things.

Albert does not dare to open his eyes. The noise in his head is getting louder.

OTHER TITLES IN THE
PETER OWEN WORLD SERIES
SEASON 3: SERBIA

MIRJANA NOVAKOVIĆ
Fear and His Servant
Translated by Terence McEneny
978-0-7206-1977-5 / 256pp / £9.99

Belgrade seems to have changed in the years since Count Otto von Hausberg last visited the city, and not for the better. Fog and mist have settled around the perimeter walls, and everywhere there is talk of murder, rebellion and death.

Serbia in the eighteenth century is a battleground of empires, with the Ottomans on one side and the Habsburgs on the other. In the besieged capital, safe for now behind the fortress walls, Princess Maria Augusta waits for love to save her troubled soul. But who is the strange, charismatic count, and can we trust the story he is telling us? While some call him the Devil, he appears to have all the fears and pettiness of an ordinary man.

In this daring and original novel, Novaković invites her readers to join the hunt for the undead, travelling through history, myth and literature into the dark corners of the land that spawned that most infamous word: vampire.

DANA TODOROVIĆ
The Tragic Fate of Moritz Tóth
Translated by the author
978-0-7206-1983-6 / 160pp / £9.99

Ex-punk Moritz Tóth is languishing in the suburbs when he receives a call from the Employment Office offering him a job as a prompter at the Opera. While trying to cope with the claustrophobia of long confinement in a rudimentary wooden box, struggling to follow Puccini's *Turandot* in a language he doesn't understand, Moritz gradually becomes convinced that he is being pursued by a malevolent force in the hideous person of his neighbour Ezekiel, a.k.a. 'the Birdman'.

In two parallel narratives — one earthly strand detailing the growing paranoia of our reluctant hero and the other, more heavenly one of Tobias Keller, the Moral Issues Adviser with the Office of the Great Overseer – the plot develops in the atmospheric style of Kafka and Bulgakov as Tobias discusses the life path of Moritz with the Disciplinary Committee. As the pieces of the puzzle finally come together and the connection between the two storylines becomes clearer, Todorović, mixing philosophy with first-class story-telling, coaxes us towards a surprising finale.

PETER OWEN WORLD SERIES
SEASON 1: SLOVENIA

JELA KREČIČ
None Like Her
Translated by Olivia Hellewell
978-0-7206-1911-9 / 288pp / £9.99
Matjaž is fearful of losing his friends over his obsession with his ex-girlfriend. To prove that he has moved on from his relationship with her, he embarks on an odyssey of dates around Ljubljana, the capital of Slovenia. In this comic and romantic tale a chapter is devoted to each new encounter and adventure. The women he selects are wildly different from one another, and the interactions of the characters are perspicuously and memorably observed.

Their preoccupations – drawn with coruscating dialogue – will speak directly to Generation Y, and in Matjaž, the hero, Jela Krečič has created a well-observed crypto-misogynist of the twenty-first century whose behaviour she offers up for the reader's scrutiny.

EVALD FLISAR
Three Loves, One Death
Translated by David Limon
978-0-7206-1930-0 / 208pp / £9.99
A family move from the city to the Slovenian countryside. The plan is to restore and make habitable a large, dilapidated farmhouse. Then the relatives arrive. There's Cousin Vladimir, a former Partisan writing his memoirs, Uncle Vinko, an accountant who would like to raise the largest head of cabbage and appear in the *Guinness World Records*, Aunt Mara and her illegitimate daughter Elizabeta who's hell bent on making her first sexual encounter the 'event of the century'. And, finally, Uncle Švejk, the accidental hero of the war for independence, turns up out of the blue one Sunday afternoon . . .

Evald Flisar handles the absurd events that follow like no other writer, making the smallest incidents rich in meaning. The house, the family, their competing instincts and desires provide an unlikely vehicle for Flisar's commentary on the nature of social cohesion and freedom.

DUŠAN ŠAROTAR
Panorama
Translated by Rawley Grau
978-0-7206-1922-5 / 208pp / £9.99
Deftly blending fiction, history and journalism, Dušan Šarotar takes the reader on a deeply reflective yet kaleidoscopic journey from northern to southern Europe. In a manner reminiscent of W.G. Sebald, he supplements his engrossing narrative with photographs, which help to blur the lines between fiction and journalism. The writer's experience of landscape is bound up in a personal yet elusive search for self-discovery, as he and a diverse group of international fellow travellers relate in their distinctive and memorable voices their unique stories and common quest for somewhere they might call home.

PETER OWEN WORLD SERIES
SEASON 2: SPAIN

CRISTINA FERNÁNDEZ CUBAS
Nona's Room
Translated by Kathryn Phillips-Miles and Simon Deefholts
978-0-7206-1953-9 / 160pp / £9.99

A young girl envious of the attention given to her sister has a brutal awakening. A young woman facing eviction puts her trust in an old lady who invites her into her home. A mature woman checks into a hotel in Madrid and finds herself in a time warp . . . In this prize-winning new collection Cristina Fernández Cubas takes us through a glass darkly into a world where things are never quite what they seem, and lurking within each of these six suspenseful short stories is an unexpected surprise. *Nona's Room* is the latest offering from one of Spain's finest contemporary writers.

JULIO LLAMAZARES
Wolf Moon
Translated by Simon Deefholts and Kathryn Phillips-Miles
978-0-7206-1945-4 / 192pp / £9.99

Defeated by Franco's Nationalists, four Republican fugitives flee into the Cantabrian Mountains at the end of the Spanish Civil War. They are on the run, skirmishing with the Guardia Civil, knowing that surrender means death. Wounded and hungry, they are frequently drawn from the safety of the wilderness into the villages they once inhabited, not only risking their lives but those of sympathizers helping them. Faced with the lonely mountains, harsh winters and unforgiving summers, it is only a matter of time before they are hunted down. Llamazares's lyrical prose vividly animates the wilderness, making the Spanish landscape as much a witness to the brutal oppression of the period as the persecuted villagers and Republicans.

Published in 1985, *Wolf Moon* was the first novel that centred on the Spanish Maquis to be published in Spain after Franco's death in 1975.

JOSÉ OVEJERO
Inventing Love
Translated by Simon Deefholts and Kathryn Phillips-Miles
978-0-7206-1949-2 / 224pp / £9.99

Samuel leads a comfortable but uninspiring existence in Madrid, consoling himself among friends who have reached a similar point in life. One night he receives a call. Clara, his lover, has died in a car accident. The thing is, he doesn't know anyone called Clara.

A simple case of mistaken identity offers Samuel the chance to inhabit another, more tumultuous life, leading him to consider whether, if he invents a past of love and loss, he could even attend her funeral. Unable to resist the chance, Samuel finds himself drawn down a path of lies until he begins to have trouble distinguishing between truth and fantasy. But such is the allure of his invented life that he is willing to persist and in the process create a new version of the present – with little regard for the consequences to himself and to others.

José Ovejero's existential tale of stolen identity exposes the fictions people weave to sustain themselves in a dehumanizing modern world.

SOME AUTHORS WE HAVE PUBLISHED

James Agee • Bella Akhmadulina • Tariq Ali • Kenneth Allsop • Alfred Andersch
Guillaume Apollinaire • Machado de Assis • Miguel Angel Asturias • Duke of Bedford
Oliver Bernard • Thomas Blackburn • Jane Bowles • Paul Bowles • Richard Bradford
Ilse, Countess von Bredow • Lenny Bruce • Finn Carling • Blaise Cendrars • Marc Chagall
Giorgio de Chirico • Uno Chiyo • Hugo Claus • Jean Cocteau • Albert Cohen
Colette • Ithell Colquhoun • Richard Corson • Benedetto Croce • Margaret Crosland
e.e. cummings • Stig Dalager • Salvador Dalí • Osamu Dazai • Anita Desai
Charles Dickens • Bernard Diederich • Fabián Dobles • William Donaldson
Autran Dourado • Yuri Druzhnikov • Lawrence Durrell • Isabelle Eberhardt
Sergei Eisenstein • Shusaku Endo • Erté • Knut Faldbakken • Ida Fink
Wolfgang George Fischer • Nicholas Freeling • Philip Freund • Carlo Emilio Gadda
Rhea Galanaki • Salvador Garmendia • Michel Gauquelin • André Gide
Natalia Ginzburg • Jean Giono • Geoffrey Gorer • William Goyen • Julien Gracq
Sue Grafton • Robert Graves • Angela Green • Julien Green • George Grosz
Barbara Hardy • H.D. • Rayner Heppenstall • David Herbert • Gustaw Herling
Hermann Hesse • Shere Hite • Stewart Home • Abdullah Hussein • King Hussein of Jordan
Ruth Inglis • Grace Ingoldby • Yasushi Inoue • Hans Henny Jahnn • Karl Jaspers
Takeshi Kaiko • Jaan Kaplinski • Anna Kavan • Yasunuri Kawabata • Nikos Kazantzakis
Orhan Kemal • Christer Kihlman • James Kirkup • Paul Klee • James Laughlin
Patricia Laurent • Violette Leduc • Lee Seung-U • Vernon Lee • József Lengyel
Robert Liddell • Francisco García Lorca • Moura Lympany • Thomas Mann
Dacia Maraini • Marcel Marceau • André Maurois • Henri Michaux • Henry Miller
Miranda Miller • Marga Minco • Yukio Mishima • Quim Monzó • Margaret Morris
Angus Wolfe Murray • Atle Næss • Gérard de Nerval • Anaïs Nin • Yoko Ono
Uri Orlev • Wendy Owen • Arto Paasilinna • Marco Pallis • Oscar Parland
Boris Pasternak • Cesare Pavese • Milorad Pavic • Octavio Paz • Mervyn Peake
Carlos Pedretti • Dame Margery Perham • Graciliano Ramos • Jeremy Reed
Rodrigo Rey Rosa • Joseph Roth • Ken Russell • Marquis de Sade • Cora Sandel
Iván Sándor • George Santayana • May Sarton • Jean-Paul Sartre
Ferdinand de Saussure • Gerald Scarfe • Albert Schweitzer
George Bernard Shaw • Isaac Bashevis Singer • Patwant Singh • Edith Sitwell
Suzanne St Albans • Stevie Smith • C.P. Snow • Bengt Söderbergh
Vladimir Soloukhin • Natsume Soseki • Muriel Spark • Gertrude Stein • Bram Stoker
August Strindberg • Rabindranath Tagore • Tambimuttu • Elisabeth Russell Taylor
Emma Tennant • Anne Tibble • Roland Topor • Miloš Urban • Anne Valery
Peter Vansittart • José J. Veiga • Tarjei Vesaas • Noel Virtue • Max Weber
Edith Wharton • William Carlos Williams • Phyllis Willmott
G. Peter Winnington • Monique Wittig • A.B. Yehoshua • Marguerite Young
Fakhar Zaman • Alexander Zinoviev • Emile Zola

Peter Owen Publishers, Conway Hall, 25 Red Lion Square, London WC1R 4RL, UK
T + 44 (0)20 7061 6756 / E info@peterowen.com
www.peterowen.com / @PeterOwenPubs
Independent publishers since 1951